RETURN
TRIPS

RETURN TRIPS

Stories by
Alice Adams

Alfred A. Knopf   New York   1985

THIS IS A BORZOI BOOK
PUBLISHED BY ALFRED A. KNOPF, INC.

Copyright © 1983, 1984, 1985 by Alice Adams

*All rights reserved under International and
Pan-American Copyright Conventions. Published
in the United States by Alfred A. Knopf, Inc.,
New York, and simultaneously in Canada by
Random House of Canada Limited, Toronto.
Distributed by Random House, Inc., New York.*

*Portions of this work originally appeared
in* The New Yorker.

"Time in Santa Fe" was first published in
San Francisco Focus; *syndicated by Fiction Network.*
*"You Are What You Own: A Notebook" was first published
in* Northeast Magazine *of the* Hartford Courant;
*syndicated by PEN. Other stories first appeared
in* Geo, Mother Jones, Ontario Review, *and* Shenandoah.

Library of Congress Cataloging in Publication Data

Adams, Alice, {date}
  Return trips.

  I. *Title.*
PS3551.D324R4 1985 813'.54 85-40116
ISBN 0-394-53633-9

Manufactured in the United States of America
First Edition

To Peter Adams Linenthal
again, with love

Contents

RETURN
TRIPS

Alaska

Although Mrs. Lawson does not drink any more, not a drop since New Year's Day, 1961, in Juneau, Alaska, she sometimes feels a confusion in her mind about which husband she will meet, at the end of the day. She has been married five times, and she has lived, it seems to her, almost everywhere. Now she is a cleaning lady, in San Francisco, although some might say that she is too old for that kind of work. Her hair, for so many years dyed red, is now streaky gray, and her eyes are a paler blue than they once were. Her skin is a dark bronze color, but she thinks of herself as Negro—black, these days. From New Orleans, originally.

If someone came up and asked her, Who are you married to now, Lucille Lawson? of course she would answer, Charles, and we live in the Western Addition in San Francisco, two busses to get there from here.

But, not asked, she feels the presences of those other husbands—nameless, shadowy, lurking near the edges of her mind. And menacing, most of them, especially the one who tromped her in Juneau, that New Year's Day. He was the worst, by far, but none of them was worth a whole lot, come to think of it. And she was always working at one place or another, and always tired, at the end of her days, and then there were those husbands to come home to, and more work to do for them. Some husbands come honking for you in their cars, she remembers, but usually you have to travel a long way, busses and street cars, to get to where they are, to where you and them live.

These days Mrs. Lawson just cleans for Miss Goldstein, a rich white lady older than Mrs. Lawson is, who lives alone in a big house on Divisadero Street, near Union. She has lots of visitors, some coming to stay, all funny-looking folk. Many foreign, but not fancy. Miss Goldstein still travels a lot herself, to peculiar places like China and Cuba and Africa.

What Mrs. Lawson is best at is polishing silver, and that is what she mostly does, the tea service, coffee service, and all the flatware, although more than once Miss Goldstein has sighed and said that maybe it should all be put away, or melted down to help the poor people in some of the places she visits; all that silver around looks boastful, Miss Goldstein thinks. But it is something for Mrs. Lawson to do every day (Miss Goldstein does not come right out and say this; they both just know).

Along with the silver polishing she dusts, and sometimes she irons a little, some silk or linen shirts; Miss Goldstein does not get dressed up a lot, usually favoring sweaters and old pants. She gets the most dressed up when she is going off to march somewhere, which she does fairly often. Then she gets all gussied up in a black suit and her real pearls, and she has these posters to carry, NO NUKES IS GOOD NUKES, GRAY PANTHERS FOR PEACE. She would be a sight to behold, Mrs. Lawson thinks: she can hardly imagine Miss Goldstein with all the kinds of folks that are usually in those lines, the beards and raggedy blue jeans, the dirty old sweat shirts, big women wearing no bras. Thin, white-haired Miss Goldstein in her pearls.

To help with the heavy housework, the kitchen floor and the stove, bathtubs and all like that, Miss Goldstein has hired a young white girl, Gloria. At first Mrs. Lawson was mistrustful that a girl like that could clean anything, a blonde-haired small little girl with these doll blue eyes in some kind of a white pants work outfit, but Gloria moves through that big house like a little bolt of white lightning, and she leaves everything behind her *clean.* Even with her eyesight not as good as it was Mrs. Lawson can see how clean the kitchen floor and the stove are, and the bathtubs. And she has *looked.*

Gloria comes at eight every morning, and she does all that in just two hours. Mrs. Lawson usually gets in sometime after nine, depending on how the busses run. And so there is some time when they are both working along, Mrs. Lawson at the sink with the silver, probably, or dusting off Miss Goldstein's bureau, dusting her books—and Gloria down on her knees on the bathroom floor (Gloria is right; the only way to clean a floor is on your knees, although not too many folks seem to know that, these days). Of course they don't talk much, both working, but Gloria has about twenty minutes before her next job, in that same neighborhood. Sometimes, then, Mrs. Lawson will take a break from her polishing, dusting, and heat up some coffee for the both of them, and they will talk a little. Gloria has a lot of worries, a lot on her mind, Mrs. Lawson can tell, although Gloria never actually says, beyond everyone's usual troubles, money and rent and groceries, and in Gloria's case car repairs, an old VW.

The two women are not friends, really, but all things considered they get along okay. Some days they don't either of them feel like talking, and they both just skim over sections of the newspaper, making comments on this and that, in the news. Other times they talk a little.

Gloria likes to hear about New Orleans, in the old days, when Mrs. Lawson's father had a drugstore and did a lot of doctoring there, and how later they all moved to Texas, and the Klan came after them, and they hid and moved again, to another town. And Gloria tells Mrs. Lawson how her sister is ashamed that she cleans houses for a living. The sister, Sharon, lives up in Alaska, but not in Juneau, where Mrs. Lawson lived. Gloria's sister lives in Fairbanks, where her husband is in forestry school.

However, despite her and Gloria getting along okay, in the late afternoons Mrs. Lawson begins to worry that Gloria will find something wrong there, when she comes first thing in the morning. Something that she, Mrs. Lawson, did wrong. She even imagines Gloria saying to Miss Goldstein, Honestly, how come you keep on that old Mrs. Lawson? She can't see to clean very good, she's too old to work.

She does not really think that Gloria would say a thing like that, and even if she did Miss Goldstein wouldn't listen, probably. Still, the idea is very worrying to her, and in an anxious way she sweeps up the kitchen floor, and dustmops the long front hall. And at the same time her mind is plagued with those images of husbands, dark ghosts, in Juneau and Oakland and Kansas City, husbands that she has to get home to, somehow. Long bus rides with cold winds at the places where you change, or else you have to wait a long time for the choked-up sound of them honking, until you get in their creaky old cars and drive, drive home, in the dark.

Mrs. Lawson is absolutely right about Gloria having serious troubles on her mind—more serious in fact than Mrs. Lawson could have thought of: Gloria's hideous, obsessive problem is a small lump on her leg, her right leg, mid-calf. A tiny knot. She keeps reaching to touch it, no matter what she is doing, and it is always there. She cannot make herself not touch it. She thinks constantly of that lump, its implications and probable consequences. Driving to work in her jumpy old VW, she reaches down to her leg, to check the lump. A couple of times she almost has accidents, as she concentrates on her fingers, reaching, what they feel as they touch her leg.

To make things even worse, the same week that she first noticed the lump Gloria met a really nice man, about her age: Dugald, neither married nor gay (a miracle, these days, in San Francisco). He is a bartender in a place where she sometimes goes with girlfriends, after a movie or something. In a way she has known Dugald for a long time, but in another way not—not known him until she happened to go into the place alone, thinking, Well, why not? I'm tired (it was late one afternoon), a beer would be nice. And there was Dugald, and they talked, and he asked her out, on his next night off. And the next day she discovered the lump.

She went with Dugald anyway, of course, and she almost had a very good time—except that whenever she thought about what was probably wrong with her she went cold and quiet. She thinks that Dugald may not ever ask her out again, and even if he did, she can't get at all involved with anyone, not now.

Also, Gloria's sister, Sharon, in Fairbanks, Alaska, has invited her to come up and stay for a week, while Sharon's forestry-student husband is back in Kansas, visiting his folks; Sharon does not much like her husband's family. Gloria thinks she will go for ten days in June, while Miss Goldstein is in China, again. Gloria is on the whole pleased at the prospect of this visit; as she Ajaxes and Lysols Miss Goldstein's upstairs bathroom, she thinks, *Alaska,* and she imagines gigantic glaciers, huge wild animals, fantastic snow-capped mountains. (She will send a friendly postcard to Dugald, she thinks, and maybe one to old Lawson.) Smiling, for an instant she makes a small bet with herself, which is that at some point Sharon will ask her not to mention to anyone, *please,* what she, Gloria, does for a living. Well, Gloria doesn't care. Lord knows her work is not much to talk about; it is simply the most money she can get an hour, and not pay taxes (she is always afraid, when not preoccupied with her other, more terrible worries, that the IRS will somehow get to her). On the other hand, it is fun to embarrass Sharon.

At home though, lying awake at night, of course the lump is all that Gloria thinks about. And hospitals: when she was sixteen she had her tonsils out, and she decided then on no more operations, no matter what. If she ever has a baby she will do it at home. The hospital was so frightening, everyone was horrible to her, all the doctors and nurses (except for a couple of black aides who were sweet, really nice, she remembers). They all made her feel like something much less than a person. And a hospital would take all her money, and more, all her careful savings (someday she plans to buy a little cabin, up near Tahoe, and raise big dogs). She thinks about something being cut off. Her leg. Herself made so ugly, everyone trying not to look. No more men, no dates, not Dugald or anyone. No love or sex again, not ever.

In the daytime her terror is slightly more manageable, but it is still so powerful that the very idea of calling a doctor, showing him the lump, asking him what to do—chills her blood, almost stops her heart.

And she can feel the lump there, all the time. Probably growing.

Mrs. Lawson has told Gloria that she never goes to doctors; she can doctor herself, Mrs. Lawson says. She always has. Gloria has even thought of showing the lump to Mrs. Lawson.

But she tries to think in a positive way about Alaska. They have a cute little apartment right on the university campus, Sharon has written. Fairbanks is on a river; they will take an afternoon trip on a paddleboat. And they will spend one night at Mount McKinley, and go on a wild life tour.

"Fairbanks, now. I never did get up that way," says Mrs. Lawson, told of Sharon's invitation, Gloria's projected trip. "But I always heard it was real nice up there."

Actually she does not remember anything at all about Fairbanks, but for Gloria's sake she hopes that it is nice, and she reasons that any place would be better than Juneau, scrunched in between mountains so steep they look to fall down on you.

"I hope it's nice," says Gloria. "I just hope I don't get mauled by some bear, on that wild life tour."

Aside from not drinking and never going to doctors (she has read all her father's old doctor books, and remembers most of what she read) Mrs. Lawson believes that she gets her good health and her strength—considerable, for a person of her years—from her daily naps. Not a real sleep, just sitting down for a while in some place really comfortable, and closing her eyes.

She does that now, in a small room off Miss Goldstein's main library room (Miss Goldstein has already gone off to China, but even if she were home she wouldn't mind about a little nap). Mrs. Lawson settles back into a big old fat leather chair, and she slips her shoes off. And, very likely because of talking about Alaska that morning, Gloria's trip, her mind drifts off, in and out of Juneau. She remembers the bitter cold, cold rains of that winter up there, the winds, fogs thicker than cotton, and dark. Snow that sometimes kept them in the little hillside cabin for days, even weeks. Her and Charles: that husband had the same name as the one she now has, she just remembered—funny to forget a thing like that. They always used to drink a lot, her and the Charles in Alaska; you had to, to get through the winter. And pretty often they would fight, ugly drunk quarrels that she couldn't quite remember the words to, in the mornings. But that New Year's Eve they were having a real nice time; he was being real nice, laughing and all, and then all of a sudden it was like he turned into some other person, and he struck her. He grabbed up her hair, all of it red, at that time, and he called her a witch and he knocked her down to the floor, and he tromped her. Later of course he was sorry, and he said he had been feeling mean about not enough work, but still, he had tromped her.

Pulling herself out of that half dream, half terrible memory, Mrs. Lawson repeats, as though someone had asked her, that now she is married to Charles, in San Francisco. They live in the Western Addition; they don't drink, and this Charles is a nice man, most of the time.

She tries then to think about the other three husbands, one in Oakland, in Chicago, in Kansas City, but nothing much comes to mind, of them. No faces or words, just shadows, and no true pictures of any of those cities. The only thing she is perfectly clear about is that not one of those other men was named Charles.

On the airplane to Alaska, something terrible, horrible, entirely frightening happens to Gloria, which is: a girl comes and sits in the seat next to hers, and that girl has—the lower part of her right leg missing. Cut off. A pretty dark-haired girl, about the same size as Gloria, wearing a nice blazer, and a kind of long skirt. One boot. Metal crutches.

Gloria is so frightened—she knows that this is an omen, a sign meant for her—that she is dizzy, sick; she leans back and closes her eyes, as the plane bumps upward, zooming through clouds, and she stays that way for the rest of the trip. She tries not to think; she repeats numbers and meaningless words to herself.

At some point she feels someone touching her arm. Flinching, she opens her eyes to see the next-seat girl, who is asking, "Are you okay? Can I get you anything?"

"I'm all right. Just getting the flu, I think." Gloria smiles in a deliberately non-friendly way. The last thing in the world that she wants is a conversation with that girl: the girl at last getting around to her leg, telling Gloria, "It started with this lump I had, right here."

Doctors don't usually feel your legs, during physical examinations, Gloria thinks; she is standing beside Sharon on the deck of the big paddleboat that is slowly ploughing up the Natoma River. It would be possible to hide a lump for a long time, unless it grew a lot, she thinks, as the boat's captain announces over the bullhorn that they are passing what was once an Indian settlement.

Alaska is much flatter than Gloria had imagined its being, at least around Fairbanks—and although she had of course heard the words, midnight sun, she had not known they were a literal description; waking at three or four in the morning from bad dreams, her nighttime panics (her legs drawn up under her, one hand touching her calf, the lump) she sees brilliant sunshine, coming in through the tattered aluminum foil that Sharon has messily pasted to the window. It is all wrong—unsettling. Much worse than the thick dark fogs that come into San Francisco in the summer; she is used to them.

In fact sleeplessness and panic (what she felt at the sight of that girl with the missing leg has persisted; she knows it was a sign) have combined to produce in Gloria an almost trancelike state. She is so quiet, so passive that she can feel Sharon wondering about her, what is wrong. Gloria does not, for a change, say anything critical of Sharon's housekeeping, which is as sloppy as usual. She does not tell anyone that she, Gloria, is a cleaning person.

A hot wind comes up off the water, and Gloria remembers that tomorrow they go to Mount McKinley, and the wild life tour.

Somewhat to her disappointment, Mrs. Lawson does not get any postcards from Gloria in Alaska, although Gloria had mentioned that she would send one, with a picture.

What she does get is a strange phone call from Gloria on the day that she was supposed to come back. What is *strange* is that Gloria sounds like some entirely other person, someone younger even than Gloria actually is, younger and perfectly happy. It is Gloria's voice, all right, but lighter and quicker than it was, a voice without any shadows.

"I'm back!" Gloria bursts out, "but I just don't think I want to work today. I was out sort of late—" She laughs, in a bright new way, and then she asks, "She's not back yet, is she?"

Meaning Miss Goldstein. "No, not for another week," Mrs. Lawson tells her. "You had a good trip?"

"Fabulous! A miracle, really. I'll tell you all about it tomorrow."

Hanging up, Mrs. Lawson has an uneasy sense that some impersonator will come to work in Gloria's place.

But of course it is Gloria who is already down on her knees, cleaning the kitchen floor, when Mrs. Lawson gets there the following day.

And almost right away she begins to tell Mrs. Lawson about the wild life tour, from Mount McKinley, seemingly the focal point of her trip.

"It was really weird," says Gloria. "It looked like the moon, in that funny light." She has a lot to say, and she is annoyed that Mrs. Lawson seems to be paying more attention to her newspaper—is barely listening. Also, Lawson seems to have aged, while Gloria was away, or maybe Gloria just forgot how old she looks, since in a way she doesn't act very old; she moves around and works a lot harder than Sharon ever does, for one example. But it seems to Gloria today that Mrs. Lawson's skin is grayer than it was, ashy-looking, and her eyes, which are always strange, have got much paler.

Nevertheless, wanting more attention (her story has an important point to it) Gloria raises her voice, as she continues, "And every time someone spotted one of those animals he'd yell out, and the man would stop the bus. We saw caribou, and these funny white sheep, high up on the rocks, and a lot of moose, and some foxes. Not any bears. Anyway, every time we stopped I got real scared. We were on the side of a really steep mountain, part of Mount McKinley, I think, and the bus was so wide, like a school bus." She does not tell Mrs. Lawson that in a weird way she liked being so scared. What she thought was, if I'm killed on this bus I'll never even get to a doctor. Which was sort of funny, really, now that she can see the humor in it—now that the lump is mysteriously, magically gone!

However, she has reached the dramatic disclosure toward which this story of her outing has been heading. "Anyway, we got back all right," she says, "and two days after that, back in Fairbanks, do you know what the headlines were, in the local paper?" She has asked this (of course rhetorical) question in a slow, deepened voice, and now she pauses, her china-blue eyes gazing into Mrs. Lawson's paler, stranger blue.

"Well, I don't know," Lawson obliges.

"They said, BUS TOPPLES FROM MOUNTAIN, EIGHT KILLED, 42 INJURED. Can you imagine? Our same bus, the very next day. What do you think that means?" This question too has been rhetorical; voicing it, Gloria smiles in a satisfied, knowing way.

A very polite woman, Mrs. Lawson smiles gently too. "It means you spared. You like to live fifty, sixty years more."

Eagerly Gloria bursts out, "Exactly! That's just the way I figured it, right away." She pauses, smiling widely, showing her little white teeth. "And then, that very same afternoon of the day we saw the paper," she goes on, "I was changing my clothes and I felt the calf of my leg where there'd been this lump that I was sort of worried about—and the lump was gone. I couldn't believe it. So I guess it was just a muscle, not anything bad."

"Them leg muscles can knot up that way, could of told you that myself," Mrs. Lawson mutters. "Heavy housework can do that to a person." But Gloria looks so happy, so bright-faced and shiny-eyed, that Mrs. Lawson does not want to bring her down, in any way, and so she adds, "But you sure are right about that bus accident. It's a sure sign you been spared."

"Oh, that's what I think too! And later we saw these really neat big dogs, in Fairbanks. I'm really thinking about getting a dog. This man I know really likes dogs too, last night we were talking." Her voice trails off in a happy reminiscence.

Later in the day, though, thinking about Gloria and her story, what she and Gloria said to each other, Mrs. Lawson is not really convinced about anything. The truth is, Gloria could perfectly well get killed by a bus in San Francisco, this very afternoon, or shot by some sniper; it's been saying in the paper about snipers, all over town, shooting folks. Or Gloria could find another lump, some place else, somewhere dangerous. Missing one bus accident is no sure sign that a person's life will always come up rosy, because nobody's does, not for long. Even Miss Goldstein, in China, could fall off of some Chinese mountain.

In a weary, discouraged way Mrs. Lawson moved through the rest of her day. It is true; she is too old and tired for the work she does. Through the big street-floor windows she watches the cold June fog rolling in from the bay, and she thinks how the weather in California has never seemed right to her. She thinks about Charles, and it comes to her that one Charles could change into the other, the same way that first Charles in such a sudden way turned violent, and wild.

That thought is enough to make her dread the end of her work, and the day, when although it is summer she will walk out into streets that are as dark and cold as streets are in Alaska.

You Are What You Own:
A Notebook

I can't leave because of all the priceless and cumbersome antique furniture that my manic mother had flown out from St. Louis—at what cost! My inheritance: it weighs me down as heavily as my feet, a part of me. Like my husband, who is also heavy, to whom I am connected, whom I cannot leave. Where do I end? And he begin? In this crazy, hot California weather we both are sticky. We are stuck.

Our house is perfectly box-shaped, the way a child would draw a house. "A real *house* house," we said, laughing at our first sight of it. We were trying to convince ourselves that we took it because it is so amusing, not because it is the only one near the university, Stanford, that we can afford. An expensive box, it costs exactly half of Carl's instructor's salary. Half the floor is living room, one-fourth kitchen, one-eighth each bathroom and bedroom. It makes a certain sense, if you think about it.

It is hard to walk through the living room, though, without bumping into something: small French tables, English desk, baroque Spanish sofa. My legs are bruised regularly. I think my mother would be surprised to see where the precious furniture has landed, crowded into a redwood box. But now she is depressed (Lithium does not work, with her), and she is not shipping any more furniture, or travelling. She does not believe in sending money.

An interesting thing about the walnut desk and the rosewood table is that they both have broken left feet. I should have called Air Express, or someone, but I wasn't sure whom, and I didn't like to complain. Mrs. Nelson, our neighbor, sighs whenever she comes over from across the street to look at the furniture, which is as often as I don't see her first and hide in bed. "Such lovely pieces," she sighs. "We've got to find a really good workman to repair them." If I told her that we couldn't afford a really good workman, she would not believe me. People with lovely furniture also have money, Mrs. Nelson believes.

So many of the people in my life seem to be over-sized. Mrs. Nelson is one of them. An enormous pale woman, large pale-blue eyes and a tight white mouth, she stands in the doorway, filling it, with her heavy arms hanging across her chest, nothing about her moving but her eyes; her gaze moves ponderously all over the room, from one broken leg to another, all over the dust, and settles at last on me. The weight of her eyes is suffocating. I become hotter and thinner and messier than I am.

"A really good workman," she says. "You can't just let nice things fall apart."

I can't?

At another time when she was manic, my mother sent me a lot of clothes, and they are what I wear, worn-out C. Klein shirts and jeans, old sweaters and skirts (A. Klein, B. Blass). My yellow hair tight in a bun. Skinny and tense, with huge, needful eyes. A group of artists lives in a big old shabby house down the block. Artists are what I believe they are. Mrs. Nelson says, sniffingly, "Gays," but to her that might mean the same. "Gay artists" surely has an attractive sound to me. In any case, they all wear beautiful bright loose clothes. I am in love, in a way, with all of them; I would like to move over there and be friends. I want to say to them, "Look, these clothes aren't really me. I ruined my only Levis in too much Clorox. I will loosen my hair and become plump and peaceful. You'll see, if you let me move in."

When Carl is at home he is often asleep; he falls asleep any- where, easily and deeply asleep. His mouth goes slack; some- times saliva seeps out, slowly, down his blond stubbled chin. Once I watched a tiny ant march heroically across Carl's face, over the wide pale planes, the thick bridge of his nose, and Carl never blinked. We have a lot of ants, especially when I leave the dishes in the sink for a couple of days, which I have recently begun to do. (Why? Am I fond of ants?) Ants crawl all over the greasy, encrusted Haviland and Spode, and the milk-fogged glasses that Mrs. Nelson refers to as my "crystal." At least that stuff sometimes breaks, whereas the furniture will surely outlast me.

I could break it?

Awake, Carl talks a lot, in his high, tight voice. And he does not say the things that you would expect of a sleepy fat blond man. He sounds like one of the other things that he is: a graduate student in psychology, with a strong side-interest in computers. He believes that he is parodying the person that he is. When I give too many clothes (all my old Norells) to the Goodwill, he says, "If only you were an anal retentive like me," thinking he is making a joke.

Carl complains, as I do, about the bulkiness of our furni- ture, the space it takes up, but I notice that he always men-

tions it, somehow, to friends who have failed to remark on
it. "A ridiculous piece of ostentation, isn't it?" he will say, not
hearing the pride in his own voice. "Helen's mother shipped
it out from St. Louis, in one of her manic phases. She's quite
immune to Lithium, poor lady."

But one Saturday he spent the whole day waxing and
polishing all the surfaces of wood. He is incredibly thorough:
for hours his fingers probed and massaged the planes and
high ornamental carvings.

How could I have married a man who looks like my mother?
How not have noticed? Although my mother's family was
all of English stock, as she puts it (thank God for my Welsh
father, although he died so young that I barely knew him),
and Carl's people are all German. Farmers, from the Sacra-
mento Valley. I thought my mother would be mad (a German peasant, from a farm), but she likes Carl. "He doesn't
seem in the least Germanic, not that they aren't a marvellous
people. He's a brilliant boy. I'm sure he'll be a distinguished
professor someday, or perhaps some fantastic computer career." And Carl asks her about the hallmarks on old silver,
and I wonder if I am alive.

I devise stratagems to keep Carl from touching me, which
sometimes he still wants to do. Unoriginally, I pretend to be
asleep, or at dinner I will begin to describe a headache or a
cramp. Or sometimes I just let him. God knows it doesn't
take long.

Carl ordered some silver polish from Macy's ($14!), silver
polish that an ad in the Chronicle said was wonderful. It
came: a whitish liquid with a ghastly sick smell. Carl spent
a perfect Saturday (for him), polishing all the silver and feeling sick.

When and why did I stop doing all the things that once absorbed my days? The washing polishing waxing of our things. When Carl said I was obsessional? No, not then. When I couldn't stand his tours of inspection? Perhaps. When I noticed that he often repolished what I had done—so unnecessary; I was an expert silver-polisher in my time. Is this my sneaky way of becoming "liberated"? (I know that I am still a long way off.)

Mrs. Nelson is obsessed with the "gay artists" down the street. (So am I, but in a different way.) There are two girls and three boys in that house, and Mrs. Nelson knows for a fact that there are only two bedrooms. So? The only time she got her face in the front door, collecting for the Red Cross (they all hooted, "We gave at the office"; not very funny, she thought), she distinctly did not see a couch where a person could sleep. So? I tell her that I don't know. I find the conversation embarrassing, and I do not mention the possibility of a rolled-up sleeping bag somewhere. Nor do I mention the nature of my own obsession with them: how do they get by with no jobs, and where (and how) did they leave whatever they used to own?

This insane climate has finally made me sick—physically, that is. In the midst of a February heat wave some dark cold wrapping rains came down upon us, rattling the windowpanes of our box-house and the palm leaves outside, and I caught a terrible cold with pleurisy and a cough, so that it seemed silly to get out of bed. Carl said he thought it was an extension of my depression (I am depressed? I thought my mother was). He told me to stay in bed, and went whistling into the kitchen to clear up dinner dishes and make breakfast.

·   ·   ·

Carl is delighted that I am sick; he is in love with all my symptoms. What does this mean? He wants me to die? No. He wants to be free to do everything that he thinks that I should do, and that he should not want to do, but he does. Yes.

I think I married Carl because he said that I should. I have always been quite docile, until I stopped washing dishes on time and polishing things—but perhaps that was further compliance. It was what Carl wanted me to do all along?

He brings in a tray. "Now, how's that for a pretty little omelet?"

Then, as suddenly as I became sick, I am well, and the rain is over and it is spring and I am in love with everyone I see: the beautiful garbage collectors and the butcher and especially the extra boy in the house down the street, who must sleep in his sleeping bag on the living room floor. He has long, pale-red hair—he is beautiful! One Saturday while Carl is polishing the silver I brush down my hair and go for a walk and there he is, the red-haired boy, saying Hi, so warmly! I walk on, after saying Hi also, but I feel that now we are friends. I give him a name—John—and from then on we have long conversations in my mind.

On another day I see a girl coming out of their yard, a dark-haired girl. We, too, say Hi to each other, and I think of her, too, as a friend, from then on. Her name is Meg, in my mind, and we, too, talk.

Looming Mrs. Nelson caught me napping. "My, your things look so *nice,* since you took to working on them," and her pale eyes glitter as though they, too, were polished. I do not tell her that it is Carl who does all that; it seems a shameful secret.

.   .   .

I point out to Carl that we would have more money if I got a job. He tells me that there are almost no jobs for anyone these days.

That is true, but it is also true that he does not want me to work.

For his computer course Carl is working on a paper. The title seems most ominous to me; it is called "The Manipulation of Data." Manipulation? *Really?* He reads paragraphs to me aloud, usually when I am reading something else. I think that Carl would like us to be more nearly interchangeable with each other, but he is becoming more and more unreal to me. I regard him from my distance, and it seems odd that we know each other, unspeakably odd that we have married.

In a charitable way I try to think of a girl who would be good for Carl, and I imagine a young girl, probably a junior in college, who is also studying psychology and computers. They could do everything together, read and cook and eat and polish everything in the house, all day long, on Saturdays.

My mother is right: Carl will be a distinguished professor. But I am surely undistinguished, as a wife.

The spring is real, though, wild and insistent: yards full of flowing acacia, fields of blossoms, and wild mustard as bright as sunshine, and light soft winds.

Mrs. Nelson sighs because there are only three stem wine glasses left, and it occurs to me how little I know about her life. Who and what was Mr. Nelson, and was she sad when he died? But it seems too late to ask.

.   .   .

I tell John and Meg (in my mind) that I think perhaps Carl and I bring out each other's worst qualities, and they agree (such wise gay artists!). I try to tell Carl that, but he says I am simply depressed. I am not depressed, really.

Watching the flowers grow, I go for many walks, smelling, breathing air. One day when I come home and find Carl asleep on the sofa, quite suddenly I am mortally stricken with pity for him, so fat and unhappy and unloved, and in that illuminated instant of real pain, I understand that he is boring because I cannot listen to him. And if I can't love him and listen, at least I could leave? I rush into the bathroom, crying, but he doesn't wake.

In my head John and Meg both say, "You could probably get *something* in the city. Or at least you'd be up there."

"But what about all the furniture?" I ask them.

"That's easy," they say.

Dear Carl,

I think we have been making each other very unhappy and that we should not do that any more, and so I am going up to San Francisco to look for a job. I took $500 from our joint account, but I will pay back half of it when I get a job. Please keep all the furniture and things, because I really don't want them any more, but don't tell Mother, in case you write to her.

Love (really),
Helen

P.S. I think it would be nice if you gave Mrs. Nelson a silver tray or a coffeepot or something.

Return Trips

Some years ago I spent a hot and mostly miserable summer in an ugly yellow hotel on the steep and thickly wooded, rocky coast of northern Yugoslavia, not far from the island of Rab. I was with a man whom I entirely, wildly loved, and he, Paul, loved me, too, but together we suffered the most excruciating romantic agonies, along with the more ordinary daily discomforts of bad food, an uncomfortable, poorly ventilated room with a hard, unyielding bed, and not enough money to get away. Or enough strength: Paul's health was bad. Morosely we stared out over the lovely clear, cool blue water, from our pine forest, to enticing islands that were purplish-gray in the distance. Or else I swam and Paul looked out after me.

Paul's problem was a congenital heart condition, now correctable by surgery, but not so then; he hurt a lot, and the smallest walks could cause pain. Even love, I came to realize, was for Paul a form of torture, although we kept at it—for him suicidally, I guess—during those endless sultry yellow afternoons, on our awful bed, between our harsh, coarse sheets.

I wanted us to marry. I was very young, and very healthy,

and my crazy, unreal idea of marriage seemed to include a sort of transfer of strength. I was not quite so silly as to consciously think that marrying me would "cure" Paul, nor did I imagine a lifelong nurse role for myself. It was, rather, a magic belief that if we did a normal thing, something other people did all the time, like getting married, Paul's heart would become normal, too, like other, ordinary hearts.

Paul believed that he would die young, and, nobly, he felt that our marriage would be unfair to me. He also pointed out that whereas he had enough money from a small inheritance for one person, himself, to live on very sparingly, there was really not enough for two, and I would do well to go back to America and to the years of graduate study to which my professor mother wanted to stake me. At that time, largely because of Paul, who was a poet, I thought of studying literature; instead, after he died I turned to history, contemporary American. By now I have written several books; my particular interest is in the Trotskyite movement: its rich history of lonely, occasionally brilliant, contentious voices, its legacy of schisms—an odd choice, perhaps, but the books have been surprisingly popular. You might say, and I hope Paul would, that I have done very well professionally. In any case you could say that Paul won our argument. That fall I went back to graduate school, at Georgetown, and Paul died young, as he said he would, in a hospital in Trieste.

I have said that Paul loved me, and so he did, intensely— he loved me more, it has come to seem to me, than anyone since, although I have had my share, I guess. But Paul loved me with a meticulous attention that included every aspect. Not only my person: at that time I was just a skinny tall young girl with heavy dark hair that was fated to early gray, as my mother's had been. With an old-fashioned name— Emma. Paul loved my hair and my name and whatever I said to him, any odd old memory, or half-formed ambition;

he took all my perceptions seriously. He laughed at all my jokes, although his were much funnier. He was even interested in my dreams, which I would sometimes wake and tell him, that summer, in the breathless pre-dawn cool, in the ugly hotel.

And so it is surprising that there was one particular dream that I did not tell him, especially since this dream was so painful and troubling that I remember it still. Much later I even arranged to reënact the dream, an expurgatory ritual of sorts—but that is to get far ahead of my story.

In the dream, then, that I dreamed as I slept with Paul, all those years ago in Yugoslavia, it was very hot, and I was walking down a long, intensely familiar hill, beside a winding white concrete highway. In the valley below was the rambling white house where (long before Yugoslavia) my parents and I had lived for almost five years, in a small Southern town called Hilton. I did not get as far as the house, in the dream; it was so hot, and I was burdened with the most terrific, heavy pain in my chest, a pain that must have come from Paul's actual pain, as the heat in the dream would have come from the actual heat of that summer.

"Oh, I had such an awful dream!" I cried out to Paul, as I burrowed against his sharp back, his fine damp skin.

"What about?" He kissed my hair.

"Oh, I don't know," I said. "I was in Hilton. You know, just before my parents' divorce. Where I had such a good time and my mother hated everything."

Against my hair he murmured, "Your poor mother."

"Yes, but she brings it on herself. She's so difficult. No wonder my father . . . really. And I don't want to go to graduate school."

And so I did not tell Paul my dream, in which I had painfully walked that downhill mile toward the scene of our

family's dissolution, and the heady start of my own ado-
lescence. Instead, in a familiar way, Paul and I argued about
my future, and as usual I took a few stray shots at my mother.

And Paul died, and I did after all go to graduate school,
and then my mother died—quite young, it now seems to me,
and long before our war was in any way resolved.

A very wise woman who is considerably older than I am
once told me that in her view relationships with people to
whom we have been very close can continue to change even
after the deaths of those people, and for me I think this has
been quite true, with my mother, and in quite another way
with Paul.

I am now going back to a very early time, long before my
summer with Paul, in Yugoslavia. Before anyone had died.
I am going back to Hilton.

When we arrived in Hilton I was eleven, and both my
parents were in their early forties, and almost everything
that went so darkly and irretrievably wrong among the
three of us was implicit in our ages. Nearly adolescent, I was
eager for initiation into romantic, sensual mysteries of which
I had dim intimations from books. For my mother, the five
years from forty-two or forty-three onward were a desolate
march into middle age. My father, about ten months younger
than my mother—and looking, always, ten years younger—
saw his early forties as prime time; he had never felt better
in his life. Like me, he found Hilton both romantic and exciting—he had a marvellous time there, as I did, mostly.

My first overtly sensual experience took place one April
night on that very stretch of road, the gravelled walk up
above the highway that wound down to our house, that I
dreamed of in Yugoslavia. I must have been twelve, and a

boy who was "walking me home" reached for and took and held my hand, and I felt an overwhelming hot excitement. Holding hands.

About hands:

These days, like most of my friends, I am involved in a marriage, my second, which seems problematical—even more problematical than most of the marriages I see—but then maybe everyone views his or her marriage in this way. Andreas is Greek, by way of Berkeley, to which his parents immigrated in the thirties and opened a student restaurant, becoming successful enough to send their promising son to college there, and later on to medical school. Andreas and I seem to go from friendliness or even love to rage, with a speed that leaves me dizzy, and scared. However, ambivalent as in many ways I am about Andreas, I do very much like— in fact, I love—his hands. They are just plain male hands, rather square in shape, usually callused and very competent. Warm. A doctor, he specializes in kidneys, unromantically enough, but his hands are more like a workman's, a carpenter's. And sometimes even now an accidental meeting of our hands can recall me to affection; his hands remind me of love.

I liked Paul's hands, too, and I remember them still. They were very smooth, and cool.

Back in Hilton, when I was twelve, my mother violently disapproved of my being out at night with boys. Probably sensing just how exciting I found those April nights that smelled of privet and lilacs, and those lean, tall, sweet-talking Southern boys, she wept and raged, despairing and helpless as she recognized the beginning of my life as a sensual woman, coinciding as it probably did with the end of her own.

My feckless father took my side, of course. "Things are different down here, my dear," he told her. "It's a scientific fact that girls, uh, mature much earlier in the South. And when in Rome, you know. I see no harm in Emma's going to a movie with some nice boy, if she promises to be home at a reasonable hour. Ten-thirty?"

"But Emma isn't Southern. She has got to be home by ten!"

My mother filled me with a searing discomfort, a longing to be away from her. Having no idea how much I pitied her, I believed that I hated her.

My father was not only younger than my mother, he was at least a full inch shorter—a small man, compactly built, and handsome. "Has anyone ever told you that you look like that writer fellow, that Scott Fitzgerald?" asked one of the local Hilton ladies, a small brunette, improbably named Popsie Hooker. "Why no, I don't believe anyone ever has," my father lied; he had been told at least a dozen times of that resemblance. "But of course I'm flattered to be compared to such a famous man. Rather a devil, though, I think I've heard," he said, with a wink at Popsie Hooker.

"Popsie Hooker, how remarkably redundant," hopelessly observed my academic mother, to my bored and restless father. They had chosen Hilton rather desperately, as a probably cheap place to live on my father's dwindling Midwestern inheritance; he was never exactly cut out for work, and after divorcing my mother he resolved his problems, or some of them, in a succession of marriages to very rich women.

Popsie Hooker, who was later to play a curious, strong role in my life, at that time interested me not at all; if I had a view of her, it was closer to my mother's than I would have admitted, and for not dissimilar reasons. She was ludicrous, so small and silly, and just a little cheap, with those girlish clothes, all ribbons and bows, and that tinny little laugh. And that accent: Popsie out-Southerned everyone around.

"It's rather like a speech defect," my mother observed, before she stopped mentioning Popsie altogether.

Aside from her smallness and blue-eyed prettiness, Popsie's local claim to fame was her lively correspondence with "famous people," to whom she wrote what were presumably letters of adulation, the puzzle being that these people so often wrote back to her. Popsie was fond of showing off her collection. She had a charming note from Mr. Fitzgerald, and letters from Eleanor Roosevelt, Norma Shearer, Willa Cather, Clare Boothe Luce. No one, least of all my mother, could understand why such people would write to dopey Popsie, nor could I, until many years later, when she began to write to me.

However, I was too busy at that time to pay much attention to my parents or their friends, their many parties at which everyone drank too much; my own burgeoning new life was much more absorbing.

My walks at night with various boys up and down that stretch of highway sometimes came to include a chaste but passionate kiss; this would take place, if at all, on the small secluded dirt road that led down from the highway to our house.

One winter, our fourth year in Hilton, when I was fifteen, in January we had an exceptionally heavy fall of snow, deep and shadowed in the valley where our house was, ladening boughs of pine and fir and entirely covering the privet and quince and boxwood that edged the highway. For several days most of the highway itself lay under snow. Cars labored up and down the hill, singly, at long intervals, wearing unaccustomed chains.

Those nights of snow were marvellous: so cold, the black sky broken with stars as white as snow. My friends and I went sledding; that winter I was strongly taken with a dark boy who looked rather like Paul, now that I try to see him: a thin, bony face, a certain Paul-like intensity. On a dare we sledded down the highway, so perilously exciting! We lay on the sled, I stretched along his back.

We went hurtling down past the back road to my house, past everything. At last on a level area we stopped; on either side of us fields of white seemed to billow and spread off into the shadows, in the cold. Standing there we kissed—and then we began the long slow ascent of the highway, toward my house. He was pulling the sled, and we stopped several times to kiss, to press our upright bodies warmly together.

As we neared and then reached the back road to my house, we saw a car stopped, its headlights on. Guiltily we dropped hands. Dazzled by the light, only as we were almost upon it could I recognize our family car, the only wood-panelled Chrysler in town. In it was my father, kissing someone; their bodies were blotted into one silhouette.

If he saw and recognized us, there was no sign. He could easily not have seen us, or, knowing my father, who was nothing if not observant, I would guess it's more likely he did see us but pretended to himself that he did not, as he pretended not to see that my mother was miserably unhappy, and that I was growing up given to emotional extremes, and to loneliness.

"Stricken" probably comes closest to how I felt: burning rage, a painful, seething shame—emotions that I took to be hatred. "I hate him" is what I thought. Oblivious of the tall boy at my side, I began to walk as fast as I could, clumping heavily through the snow; at the door of my house I muttered what must have been a puzzlingly abrupt good night. Without kissing.

By the time we left Hilton, the summer that I was sixteen, my parents were entirely fed up with Hilton, and with each other. My father thought he could get a job in the Pentagon, in Washington—he knew someone there; and my mother had decided on New York, on graduate school at Columbia; I would go to Barnard.

I was less upset about my parents' separation than I was about leaving Hilton, which was by now to me a magic, enchanted place. In the spring and summer just preceding our departure there were amazing white bursts of dogwood, incredible wisteria and roses.

I wept for my friends, whom I would always love and miss, I thought.

I hated New York. The city seemed violent and confusing, ugly and dirty, loud. Voices in the streets or on subways and busses grated against my ears; everyone spoke so stridently, so harshly. Until I met Paul I was lonely and miserable, and frightened.

I would not have told him of my unease right away, even though Paul and I began as friends. But he must have sensed some rural longings just beneath my New York veneer. He would have; almost from the start Paul felt whatever I felt—he came to inhabit my skin.

In any case, our friendship and then our love affair had a series of outdoor settings. Paul, melancholy and romantic, and even then not well, especially liked the sea, and he liked to look out to islands—which led us, eventually, to Yugoslavia, our desolate summer there.

Not having had an actual lover before, only boys who kissed me, who did not talk much, I was unprepared for the richness of love with Paul—or, rather, I assumed that that was how love was between true intimates. Paul's sensuality was acutely sensitive, and intense; with him I felt both beautiful and loved—indescribably so. You could say that Paul spoiled me for other men, and in a way that is true—he did.

But on the other hand Paul knew that he was dying, gradually, and that knowledge must have made him profligate with love. We talked and talked, we read poetry; Paul read Wallace Stevens and Eliot aloud to me, and his own poems, which I thought remarkable. We made jokes, we laughed, we made love.

Since Hilton was only twelve hours from New York by train, and we both liked travel, and trains, in a way it is odd that Paul and I did not go down to Hilton. I know he would have said yes had I suggested a trip. His curiosity about me was infinite; he would have wanted to see a place that I cared so much about. I suppose we would have stayed at the inn, as I was to do later on, when finally I did go back to Hilton. We could have taken a taxi out to what had been my house.

However, for whatever reasons, Paul and I did not go to Hilton. We went to upstate New York and to Connecticut, and out to Long Island.

And, eventually, to Yugoslavia.

Our unhappiness there in the ugly yellow hotel on the beautiful rockbound coast was due not only to Paul's declining health and my unreal but urgent wish to marry. Other problems lay in the sad old truth, well known to most adults but not at that time to us, that conducting a love affair while living apart is quite unlike taking up residence together, even for a summer. In domestic ways we were both quite impossible then—and of course Paul did not get time to change.

I could not cook, and our arrangement with the hotel included the use of a communal kitchen, an allotted space in the refrigerator and time at the stove; my cooking was supposed to save us money, which my burned disasters failed to do. Neither could I sew or iron. I even somehow failed at washing socks. None of this bothered Paul at all; his expectations of me did not run along such lines, but mine, which must have been plucked from the general culture rather than from my own freethinking mother, were strong, and tormenting.

Paul had terrible troubles with the car, a Peugeot that we had picked up in Paris, on our way, and that had functioned perfectly well all across the Italian Alps, until we got to Trieste, where it began to make inexplicable noises, and sometimes not to start. Paul was utterly incapable of dealing with these *crises;* he would shout and rant, even clutch melodramatically at his thin black hair. I dimly sensed that he was reacting to the car's infirmities instead of to his own, which of course I did not say; but I also felt that men were supposed to deal with cars, an insupportable view, I knew even then, and derived from my father, who possessed remarkable mechanical skills.

We were there in Yugoslavia for almost three months in all, from June to September. It was probably in August, near the end of our stay, that I had my dream of going back to Hilton, and walking down the highway to our house—in the heat, with the pain in my heart that must have been Paul's pain. The dream that I did not tell Paul.

And in the fall I went back to America, to Washington, D.C., to study at Georgetown.

And Paul moved up to Trieste, where shortly after Christmas he went into a hospital and died.

Sheer disbelief was my strongest reaction to the news of Paul's death, which came in the form of a garbled cablegram. I could not believe that such an acute and lively intelligence could simply be snuffed out. In a conventional way I wept and mourned his loss: I played music that he had liked—the Hummel trumpet concerto, of which he was especially fond —and I reread "Sunday Morning" and "Four Quartets." But at the same time I never believed that he was entirely gone (I still do not).

Two years after Paul's death, most unexpectedly my
mother died, in a senseless automobile accident; she was
driving to see friends in Connecticut and swerved on a wet
highway to avoid an oncoming truck. I was more horrified,
more devastated, really, than I could have believed possible.
I went to an analyst. "I haven't even written her for a
month!" I cried out, during one dark fifty-minute hour. "How
many letters does it take to keep a mother alive?" was the
gentle and at least mildly helpful answer. Still, I wrestled
with my guilt and with the sheer irresolution of our connection for many, many years.

In my late twenties I married one of my former professors:
Lewis—a large, blond, emphatically healthy, outgoing man,
as much unlike Paul as anyone I could have found; this occurred to me at the time as an ironic twist that only Paul
himself could have appreciated. We lived in New York,
where we both now taught.

To sum up very complicated events in a short and simple
way: my work prospered, while my marriage did not—and
I present these as simultaneous conditions, not causally linked.
A happier first marriage could have made for even better
work on my part, I sometimes think.

During those years, I thought of my mother with increasing sympathy. This is another simplification, but that is what
it came to. She did her best under very difficult, sometimes
painful circumstances is one way of putting it.

And I thought of Paul. It was his good-friend aspect that
I most missed, I found, in the loneliness of my marriage. I
felt, too, always, the most vast regret for what seemed the
waste of a life.

And Hilton was very much in my mind.

Sometimes I tried to imagine what my life would have
been like if I had never left: I could have studied at the
university there, and married one of those lean and sexy

sweet-talking boys. And often that seemed a preferable way to have taken.

I divorced Lewis, and I had various "relationships." I wrote and published articles, several books—and I began getting letters from Popsie Hooker. Long, quite enthralling letters. They were often about her childhood, which had been spent on a farm in Illinois—southern Illinois, to be sure, but, still, I thought how my mother would have laughed to hear that Popsie, the near-professional Southerner, was really from Illinois. Popsie wrote to me often, and I answered, being compulsive in that way, and also because I so much enjoyed hearing from her.

Some of her letters were very funny, as when she wrote about the new "rest home" in Hilton, in which certain former enemies were housed in adjacent rooms: "Mary Lou and Henrietta haven't spoken for years and *years,* and there they are. Going over there to visit is like reading a novel, a real long one," Popsie wrote, and she added, "They couldn't get me into one of those places if they carried me there on a stretcher." I gathered that Popsie was fairly rich; several husbands had come and gone, all leaving her well endowed.

We wrote back and forth, Popsie and I, she writing more often than I did, often telling me how much my letters meant to her. Her letters meant a great deal to me, too. I was especially moved when she talked about the seasons down there in Hilton—the weather and what was in bloom; I could remember all of it, so vividly. And I was grateful that she never mentioned my parents, and her own somewhat ambiguous connection with them.

During some of those years, I began an affair with Andreas, the doctor whom I eventually married: a turbulent, difficult, and sometimes rewarding marriage. Andreas is an exceptionally skilled doctor; he is also arrogant, quick-tempered, and inconsiderate, especially of other people's time—like all doctors, I have sometimes thought.

Our conflicts often have to do with schedules: his conference in Boston versus mine in Chicago; his need for a vacation in February versus mine for time to finish a book, just then. And more ordinary arguments: my dislike of being kept waiting, his wish that I do more cooking. Sometimes even now his hot, heavy body next to mine in bed seems alien, unknown, and I wonder what he is doing there, really. At other times, as I have said, I am deeply stirred by an accidental touching of our hands.

At some of our worst moments I think of leaving Andreas; this would be after an especially ugly quarrel, probably fuelled by too much wine, or simply after several weeks of non-communication.

In one such fantasy I do go back to Hilton, and I take up the rest of my life there as a single woman. I no longer teach, I only do research in the library, which is excellent. And I write more books. I imagine that I see a lot of Popsie Hooker; I might even become the sort of "good daughter" to her that I was so far from being to my own mother. And sometimes in this fantasy I buy the house that we used to live in, the rambling house down the highway, in the valley. I have imagined it as neglected, needing paint, new gutters, perhaps even falling apart, everything around it overgrown and gone to seed.

Last June, when I had agreed to give a series of lectures at Georgetown, Andreas and I made reservations in a small hotel where we had stayed before, not far from the university. We both like Washington; we looked forward to revisiting favorite galleries and restaurants. It was one of the many times when we needed a vacation together, and so, as I might have known would happen, this became impossible:

two sick patients got sicker, and although I argued, citing the brilliance and the exceptional competence of his partners (an argument that did not go over very well), Andreas said no, he had to stay in New York, with the kidneys of Mrs. Howell · and old Mr. Rosenthal.

I went to Georgetown and to our hotel alone. I called several times, and Andreas and I "made up" what had been a too familiar argument.

In Georgetown, the second day, as I walked alone past those elegantly maintained houses, as I glanced into seductively cloistered, luxuriantly ferned and flowered gardens, some stray scent of privet or a glimpse of a yellow rosebush in full bloom—something reminded me strongly, compellingly of Hilton, and I thought, Well, why not? I could take the train and just stay for a couple of days. That much more time away from Andreas might be to the good, just now. I could stay at the Hilton Inn. I could visit Popsie. I could walk down the highway to our house.

And that is what I did, in more or less that order, except that I saved the visit to Popsie for the last, which turned out to be just as well. But right away I stopped at a travel agency on Wisconsin Avenue, and I bought a ticket to Raleigh, treating myself to a roomette for the five-hour trip; I felt that both ceremony and privacy were required.

I had thought that on the train I would be struck by the deep familiarity of the landscape; at last, that particular soil, that special growth. But actually it was novelty that held me to my window: the wide flat brown shining rivers that we crossed, with their tacky little marinas, small boats, small boys on the banks. Flooded swamps, overgrown with kudzu vines and honeysuckle. I had the curious illusion that one sometimes gets on trains, of traversing an exotic, hitherto untravelled land. I felt myself to be an explorer.

That night I had an unmemorable dinner alone at the inn
—which, having been redone, was all unfamiliar to me. I
went to bed early, slept well.

Sometime in the night, though, I did wake up with the
strange and slightly scary thought that in a few years I would
be as old as my mother was when she died, and I wondered
what, if anything, that fact had to do with my coming back
to Hilton, after all these years.

The next morning's early air was light and delicate. Dew
still shone on the heavy, dark-green shrubbery around the
inn, on silver cobwebs, as I set out for my walk—at last!
The sky was soft and pale, an eggshell blue. Walking along
the still gravelled sidewalk, beside the tarred road that led
from the inn out to the highway, I recognized houses; I knew
who used to live in almost all of them, and I said those names
to myself as I walked along: Hudson, Phipps, Zimmerman,
Rogerson, Pittman. I noticed that the old Pittman place was
now a fraternity house, with an added sun porch and bright
new paint, bright gold Greek letters over the door. In fact,
the look of all those houses was one of improvement, up-
grading, with their trim lawns, abundant boxwood, their
lavish flower beds.

I reached the highway, still on the gravelled walk, and I
began the long descent toward my house. The air was still
light, and barely warm, although the day to come would be
hot. I thought of my dream in Yugoslavia, of this walk, and
I smiled, inexplicably happy at just that moment—with no
heat, no pain in my heart.

I recognized more houses, and said more names, and I
observed that these houses, too, were in splendid shape, all
bright and visibly cared for. There was much more green
growth than I remembered, the trees were immense, and I
thought, Well, of course; they've had time to grow.

No one seeing me as I walked there could know or guess that that was where I used to live, I thought. They would see —a tall thin woman, graying, in early middle age, in a striped gray cotton skirt, gray shirt. A woman looking intently at everything, and smiling to herself.

And then, there before me was our house. But not our house. It, too, had been repainted—all smartened up with bright white paint and long black louvred shutters, now closed against the coming heat and light. Four recent-model sports cars, all imported, were parked in the driveway, giving the place a recreational, non-familiar air. A group of students, I thought; perhaps some club? The surrounding trees were huge; what had been a small and murmurous pine grove at one side of the house now towered over it, thickly green and rustling slightly in a just-arisen morning breeze. No one came out while I stood there, for not very long, but I was sure that there was not a family inside but some cluster of transients—young people, probably, who liked each other and liked the house, but without any deep or permanent attachment.

I continued on my walk, a circle of back roads on which I was pleased to find that I still knew my way, which led at last back to the highway, and up the hill, to the inn.

I had called Popsie Hooker from Washington, and again from the inn, when I got there. She arose from her nap about four in the afternoon, she said, and if I could come out to her house along about then she would be thrilled, just simply thrilled.

By midafternoon it was too hot for another walk, and so I took a taxi out to Popsie's house, in the direction opposite to mine. I arrived about four-thirty, which I assumed to be along about four in Southernese.

Popsie's house, the fruit of one of her later marriages, was by far the most splendid I had yet seen in town: a Georgian house, of ancient soft red brick smartly trimmed in black, with frequent accents of highly polished brass. Magnificent lawns, magnolias, rhododendrons. By the time I got to the door I half expected to be greeted by an array of uniformed retainers—all black, of course.

But it was Popsie herself who opened the door to me—a Popsie barely recognizable, so shrunken and wizened had she become: a small woman withered down to dwarf size, in a black silk dress with grosgrain at her throat, a cameo brooch. She smelled violently of gardenia perfume and of something else that at first I could not place.

"Emma! Emma!" she breathed up into my face, the old blue eyes filming over, and she caught at both my arms and held them in her weak tight grasp. I recognized the second scent, which was sherry.

"You're *late*," she next accused me. "Here I've been expecting you this whole long after*noon.*"

I murmured apologies, and together we proceeded down the hallway and into a small parlor, Popsie still clutching my arm, her small fierce weight almost tugging me over sideways.

We sat down. The surfaces in that room were all so cluttered with silver and ivory pieces, inlay, old glass, that it could have been an antique shop, or the parlor of a medium. I told Popsie how happy I was to be there, how wonderful Hilton looked.

"Well, you know, it's become a very fancy place to live. Very *expensive.* Lots of Yankees retiring down here, and fixing up the old houses."

"Uh, where do the poor people live?"

She laughed, a tiny rasp. "Oh, there you go, talking *liberal,* and you just got here. Well, the poor folks, what's left of them, have moved out to Robertsville."

Robertsville was the adjacent town, once predominantly black, and so I next asked, "What about the Negroes?"

"Well, I guess they've just sort of drifted back into the countryside, where they came from. But did you notice all the fancy new stores on Main Street? All the restaurants, and the *clothes?*"

We talked for a while about the new splendors of Hilton, and the rudeness of the new Yankees, who did not even go to church—as I thought, This could not be the woman who has been writing to me. Although of course she was—the same Popsie, half tipsy in the afternoon; she probably spent her sober mornings writing letters. This woman was more like the Popsie of my early years in Hilton, that silly little person, my mother's natural enemy.

Possibly to recall the Popsie of the wonderful letters, I asked about the local rest home. How were things out there?

"Well, I have to tell you. What gripes me the most about that place is that they don't pay any taxes" was Popsie's quick, unhelpful response. "Tax-*free*, and you would not believe the taxes I have to pay on this old place."

"But this place is so beautiful." I did not add, And you have so much money.

"Well, it is right pretty," she acknowledged, dipping her head. "But why must I go on and on paying for it? It's not fair."

Our small chairs were close together in that crowded, stuffy room, so that when Popsie leaned closer yet to me, her bleary eyes peering up into mine, the sherry fumes that came my way were very strong indeed. And Popsie said, "You know, I've always thought you were so beautiful, even if no one else ever thought you were." She peered again. "Where did you get that beauty, do you think? Your mother never was even one bit pretty."

More stiffly than I had meant to, I spoke the truth. "Actually I look quite a lot like my mother," I told her. And I am not beautiful.

Catching a little of my anger, which probably pleased her, Popsie raised her chin. "Well, one thing certain, you surely don't favor your daddy."

"No, I don't. I don't favor him at all." My father had recently moved to La Jolla, California, with another heiress, this one younger than I am, which would have seemed cruel news to give to Popsie.

After a pause, during which I suppose we both could have been said to be marshalling our forces, Popsie and I continued our conversation, very politely, until I felt that I could decently leave.

I told her how much I liked her letters, and she said how she liked mine, and we both promised to write again, very soon—and I wondered if we would.

On the plane to New York, a smooth, clear, easy flight, I was aware of an unusual sense of well-being, which out of habit I questioned. I noted the sort of satisfaction that I might have been expected to feel on finishing a book, except that at the end of books I usually feel drained, exhausted. But now I simply felt well, at peace, and ready for whatever should come next.

Then Paul returned from nowhere to my mind, more strongly than for some time. In an affectionate way I remembered how impossible he was, in terms of daily life, and how much I had loved him—and how he had loved me.

Actually he and Andreas were even more unlike than he and Lewis were, I next thought, and a little wearily I noted my own tendency to extremes, and contrasts. Andreas likes to fix and mend things, including kidneys, of course. He is good with cars. "I come from strong Greek peasant stock" is a thing that he likes to say, and it is true; clearly he does, with his powerful black hair, his arrogant nose. His good strong heart.

We were planning a trip to Greece the following fall. Andreas had gone back as a boy to visit relatives, and later with both his first and second wives. And he and I had meant to go, and now we would.

We planned to fly to Rome, maybe spend a few days there; we both like Rome. But now another route suggested itself: we could fly to Vienna, where we have never been, and then take the train to Trieste, where we could pick up a car and drive down to Greece by way of Yugoslavia. We would drive past the ferry to the island of Rab, and past the road that led to our yellow hotel. I did not imagine driving down to see it; Andreas would be in a hurry, and my past does not interest him much. He would see no need to stop on such an errand.

Nor do I. And besides, that particular ugly, poorly built structure has probably been torn down. Still, I very much like the idea of just being in its vicinity.

La Señora

The grand hotel is some kilometres beyond the village, on a high road that winds between the jungle and the sea. It has been there for years now, standing taller than the palm trees that surround it, the fat-trunked palms all wrapped with flower vines.

The face of this hotel has many balconies with small fringed awnings, and everywhere windows, all wide and open to the air. Even the dining room, the largest of all rooms and by far the most grand, looks out openly to the sea.

Some of the village girls work there as waitresses. They are very pretty girls, but silly, most of them, and not serious in their work. Older women, if they still are strong, with luck may obtain positions as room maids. Those maids have in their care the rows of large and very beautiful rooms where the hotel guests come to live—the gringos, from everywhere up north. The room maids also have charge of all the sheets and towels, each day supplying more to each room, all fresh and clean. They dust out the rooms, those maids, even sweeping under the beds, if they choose to do so.

The room maids in most respects are more fortunate than the dining room girls. The work of the girls is harder, which is just, since they are much younger, and their wages are somewhat higher; but often the room maids have closer associations with the guests, some of whom are especially kind, in terms of tips and presents. Many guests come year after year and often to their exact same rooms, each year, and they remember the names of the maids—though often pronouncing them strangely, and confusing Teodola with Teodora, for example. Naturally some other guests are not at all sympathetic, with their floors full of wet towels and sand, their strong-smelling bottles and broken glasses, their stains of lipstick, dark smudges on sheets, pillowcases.

There is one guest, a very thin and now very old North American, a woman who came there always with her husband and then for a time alone, a lady always referred to by the maids and even the silliest dining room girls as La Señora, always said in a certain way, "La Señora," so that only this lady is meant.

She is very white, the señora, everything white, her skin and her hair like white silk and almost all of her clothes. She is white, but with great dark eyes, like Mexican eyes. Despite all her years this lady moves very swiftly, and with great smoothness; she might balance a jug of water on her head, and never spill. She is kind, this lady, but at times she can be fiercely angry, when she feels that what has been done is not quite right. Many of the maids greatly fear her, and dread her coming; she was even heard to raise her voice in a harsh way with her husband.

With Teodola, though, the oldest room maid, the one who has been there longest, the lady has never been angry. To Teodola it seems that they have a way of understanding each other. She, Teodola, understands that it is important to the lady that the floors of the room all be dusted, even under the beds; that the sheets on the bed be stretched tight; and that all of the white parts of the bathroom be washed many, many times. And the lady understands that Teodola does not like to be cálled Teodora, and that inquiries as to her health are received as great courtesies. The lady brings large boxes of chocolates to Teodola; Teodola does not eat candy any longer but she enjoys handing it out to her grandchildren.

Each year the lady brings her dictionary of Spanish words, and each year she speaks more, and she seems better able to understand Teodola. In the mornings after taking her breakfast the lady always sits for a time on the terrace of her room, in former years with her husband (whom now Teodola has almost forgotten, as even her own dead husband has dimmed in her mind), in recent years alone. She reads from books, she writes in another small book, she writes on postcards. But she seems for most hours just to rest there, to regard the flowers that border her terrace, the bushes and vines; the pink, red, purple blossoms, white butterflies, black hummingbirds. The far-off sea.

In her own late years Teodola is often unclear as to seasons, except to observe that the weather, which should never change, now does so; there is rain, even coolness, quite unexpectedly. There is thus no seasonal way for her to know precisely the day of the arrival of the lady, except that she does know: her dreams inform her. She begins to dream of the lady, several nights of such dreams, and then there will come a morning when she knocks on a certain door—and there is *La Señora*, the very white lady in her light white clothes, embracing Teodola—a small quick light kiss on each cheek, like the kiss of a bird—and the lady saying, "Ah, Teodola, well, here I am again. I never believe I'm going to make it ever again, but here I am. And how happy I am to see you! You look very well—you have had a good year? Your health has been good—and your children? Tell me, how many grandchildren by now? Please, I want you to say all their names to me."

And Teodola will begin to recite: "Ernesto, Felipe, Sara, Elvira, Carlos, Eva. And the infant Jimenez, Jimmy." Then both she and the lady will laugh from sheer happiness, Teodola being happy to see the lady again, the lady who now will be there for quite a while; and the lady, who is every year more white, and smaller in her bones, is happy to be resting in the warm bright days, to be watching her birds and flowers, and the gold-blue ocean waves.

There must come a year when the lady does not appear; this is something that Teodola has considered. The lady is very old: one day she must die. What Teodola does not know is in what way she herself will receive this information. It is possible that she will simply dream of the death of the lady, but even if such a dream did come she would not quite trust it, for lately she has received information from dreams that is quite unreliable. She has seen her husband alive again, and wanting more sons, wanting ever more sons, and she has dreamed of her grandchildren old and dying in wars—all craziness.

But someday the lady will be permanently gone, and in the meantime Teodola's own days go faster and faster, always less time between dawn, the moment of leaving her hut just outside the village, and sunset, the long tired downhill homeward trudge.

Teodola is much respected by the other room maids. They respect her right to private naps, sometimes, in an unused room just next to the storeroom of linens. They do not ask that she carry the largest stacks of clean sheets, or full trays of new glasses. They even (usually) obey her when Teodola says that a certain floor must be dusted yet once again, especially in the room of the señora, who at any moment could still reappear. The maids and the girl waitresses too all respect

Teodola, but they do not have true friendship for her; to them Teodola seems just a woman alone, become old and strange. Teodola knows of their feelings, but such isolation is a part of becoming old that one must accept, she believes.

However, on a certain day all the waitress girls and the hotel maids together decide to play a trick on Teodola, a trick that is at last too much for her.

It begins quite early one morning, when Teodola is walking slowly up the steep dirt road, all crevassed and full of holes, toward the main hotel road, and on her way she encounters a very young and pretty waitress girl, Elisabeta, who says to her, "Oh Teodola, have you heard the news? La Señora does not come this year. She has died up in the north, in New York."

Teodola experiences a sharp sudden pain, but she frowns, refusing to be teased in this way, and by this particularly foolish girl, who is always much too familiar with the manager. "You know nothing," she tells the girl. "You are so silly, believing whatever a man says to you!"

Elisabeta makes an angry face, but she hurries away without more lying.

But later on that same day when Teodola insists that one of the room maids, Margarita, again dust the floor of the room of the lady, Margarita simply stares at Teodola and asks her, "But why, Teodola? Why dust the floor? You know that we have heard that the lady is dead."

Although it is not yet noon the sun is especially hot, and Teodola already is very tired; she had just been thinking of her coming nap. Perhaps for those reasons she is crosser than she intended to be with Margarita. "Enough of your teasing and laziness!" she cries out. "You say anything that arrives in your head to avoid doing work. You tell lies!"

Margarita shakes her head in an angry way, as Teodola recalls that she, Margarita, is the aunt of Elisabeta: of course, it is a story that the two of them together have concocted, for tormenting Teodola.

Teodola herself then sets about dusting the floor in the room of the lady, and that work is a comfort to her. As always, she feels the presence of the lady there; she can almost smell the flower-sweet scent of the lady's clothes, can almost hear the sound of the lady's voice, as she tries new Spanish words.

In the afternoon of that day two other maids try the same trick on Teodola, both of them saying, "Teodola, did you hear? La Señora has died." But by now Teodola knows not to say anything whatsoever, not to gratify them by her anger, nor to show that she knows that they lie. She ignores them; she does her work of making the beds and arranging the flowers in all the bedside tables. Those words have given her a queasy feeling, though, an inner blackness.

At the end of the day, the huge red sun slipping down below the line of the darkening sea, Teodola starts home. The walk seems much longer and harder than usual, but at last she arrives at her hut. Too tired to eat, she lies down on her mattress, and is soon fast asleep.

Night comes without her waking, and with it strange dreams. In one of them the señora has indeed arrived at the hotel but she herself, Teodola, has died. Very strange indeed: within the dream Teodola knows that she is dreaming, and that nothing in the dream is true—of course if she were dead she would not be dreaming. Yet when she struggles very hard to wrest herself from sleep and from the dream, she cannot. She is powerless against her sleep, against the dream.

New Best Friends

"The McElroys really don't care about seeing us anymore—aren't you aware of that?" Jonathan Ferris rhetorically and somewhat drunkenly demands of his wife, Sarah Stein.

Evenly she answers him, "Yes, I can see that."

But he stumbles on, insisting, "We're low, *very* low, on their priority list."

"I *know*."

Jonathan and Sarah are finishing dinner, and too much wine, on one of the hottest nights of August—in Hilton, a mid-Southern town, to which they moved (were relocated) six months ago; Jonathan works for a computer corporation. They bought this new fake-Colonial house, out in some scrubby pinewoods, where now, in the sultry, sulfurous paralyzing twilight no needle stirs, and only mosquitoes give evidence of life, buzz-diving against the window screens.

In New York, in their pretty Bleecker Street apartment, with its fern-shaded courtyard, Sarah would have taken Jonathan's view of the recent McElroy behavior as an invitation to the sort of talk they both enjoyed: insights, analyses—and, from Sarah, somewhat literary speculations. Their five-year marriage has always included a great deal of talk, of just this sort.

However, now, as he looks across the stained blond maple table that came, inexorably, with the bargain-priced house, across plates of wilted food that they were too hot and tired to eat—as he focusses on her face Jonathan realizes that Sarah, who never cries, is on the verge of tears; and also that he is too drunk to say anything that would radically revise what he has already said.

Sarah does begin to cry. "I know we're low on their list," she chokes. "But after all we only met them a couple of months before they moved away. And they'd always lived here. They have family, friends. I've always accepted that. I even said it to you. So why do you have to point it out?"

If he could simply get to his feet, could walk around the table and say, I'm sorry, I didn't mean it—then at least temporarily there would be an improvement in the air between them, a lifting of the heavy night's burden. But Jonathan cannot move; it is so hot his shirt is still stuck to his back, as it has been all day. And he is exhausted.

Besides, what he just said about the McElroys (who at first seemed an instrument of salvation; Sarah was crazy about them) is all too true: Hugh and Hattie McElroy, who moved to Santa Fe in June, now are back for the wedding of a son, and Sarah has barely seen them. And she used to see Hattie almost every day. On this visit, though, the McElroys have come to Sarah and Jonathan's once for dinner, and Sarah saw Hattie at a large lunch party (given by Hattie's old friend Popsie Hooker).

Of course, having lived here forever, the McElroys are indeed involved with family and friends, as Sarah has just said. But really, Jonathan now furiously thinks (as Sarah must have thought), at least they could call her; they could meet for tea, or something.

Weeping, Sarah looks blotchy, aged, distorted; her fine, just-not-sharp features are blurred. "Piquant" is the word that Jonathan's mother has found for Sarah's face. "Well, I wouldn't call her pretty, in any conventional way, but her face is so intelligent, so—piquant." To Jonathan, her face is simply that, her own; he is so close to her that he rarely thinks about it, except that a sudden, unexpected sight of her can deeply move him still. She simply looks like a young woman who is crying, almost any young woman.

Thinking this, it occurs to Jonathan that he has never seen another man cry, and he himself would like to weep, at this moment; it is so hot, they are both so unhappy, everything seems lost. He pulls himself together, though, after this frightening thought, and then he remembers that in fact he did see his own father in tears, as he lay dying, in Mass. General Hospital; big heavy tears ran down his father's long lined white face.

"You must think I'm really stupid," Sarah gets out.

No, you're the brightest girl I ever met, Jonathan does not say. Nor does he add, But that was a stupid remark.

Stupid is the last thing that Sarah is, actually, and during their New York married life (before *this*) she had no trouble getting the part-time editorial jobs that she liked, or books to review. Those occupations used to absorb much of Sarah's time, and her plentiful energy, and Jonathan knows that lack of any such work down here contributes to her unhappiness; it is not just disappointment with the McElroys.

In New York, in a vague, optimistic way (they have been generally happy people, for these times), as they discussed the projected move to Hilton, Sarah and Jonathan assured each other that since it was a university town, not just any old backward Southern city, there would be work of some sort available to her, at the university press, or somewhere. Saying which they forgot one crucial fact, which is that in or around any university there are hundreds of readily exploitable bright students' wives, or students, who grasp at all possible, however low-paying, semi-intellectual work.

And so for Sarah there has been little to do, in the too large, uncharming house, which (Jonathan has unhappily recognized) Sarah has been keeping much too clean. All her scrubbing and waxing, her dusting and polishing have a quality of desperation, as well as being out of character; his old busy Sarah was cheerfully untidy, which was quite all right with Jonathan, who did not mind housework.

Unsteadily, they now clear the table and wash up. They go upstairs to bed; they try to sleep, in the thick damp heat.

Sarah and Jonathan's first month in Hilton, February, was terrible for them both. Cold, dark and windy, and wet, a month of almost unrelenting rains, which turned the new red clay roads leading out to their house into tortuous slicks, deeply rutted, with long wide puddles of muddy red water, sometimes just frozen at the edges. Cold damp drafts penetrated their barnlike house; outside, in the woods, everything dripped, boughs sagged, and no birds sang.

March was a little better: not yet spring, none of the promised balmy Southern blue, and no flowers, but at least the weather cleared; and the blustery winds, though cold, helped to dry the roads, and to cleanse the air.

And, one night at dinner, Sarah announced that she had met a really wonderful woman, in a bookstore. "My new best friend," she said, with a tiny, half-apologetic laugh, as Jonathan's heart sank, a little. They both knew her tendency toward somewhat ill-advised enthusiasms: the charming editor who turned out to be a lively alcoholic, given to midnight (and later) phone calls; the smart young film critic who made it instantly clear that she hated all their other friends. The long line of initially wonderful people, the new best friends, who in one way or another became betrayers of Sarah's dreams of friendship.

However, there was another, larger group of friends she'd had for years, who were indeed all that Sarah said they were, smart and loyal and generous and fun. Jonathan liked those friends, now his friends, too. Life with Sarah had, in fact, made him more gregarious, changing him from a solitary, overeducated young man with a boring corporation job, despite an advanced degree in math, into a warmer, friendlier person. Sarah's talkative, cheery friends were among her early charms for Jonathan. He simply wondered at her occasional lapses in judgment.

Hattie McElroy, the new best friend (and the owner, it turned out, of the bookstore where they had met), was very Southern, Sarah said; she was from Hilton. However, except for her accent (which Sarah imitated, very funnily), she did not seem Southern. "She reads so much, I guess it gives her perspective," Sarah said. And, with a small pleased laugh, "She doesn't like it here very much. She says she's so tired of everyone she knows. They're moving to Santa Fe in June. Unfortunately, for me."

After that, all Sarah's days seemed to include a visit to Hattie's bookstore, where Hattie served up mugs of tea, Sarah said, along with "super" gossip about everyone in town. "There's an old group that's unbelievably stuffy," Sarah reported to Jonathan. "People Hattie grew up with. They never even want to meet anyone new. Especially Yankees." And she laughed, happy to have such an exclusive connection with her informative and amusing new friend.

"Any chance you could take over the bookstore when they leave?" asked Jonathan, early on. "Maybe we could buy it?" This was during the period of Sarah's unhappy discovery about the work situation in Hilton, the gradually apparent fact of there being nothing for her.

"Well, the most awful thing. She sold it to a chain, and just before we got here. She feels terrible, but she says there didn't seem any other way out, no one else came around to buy it. And the chain people are even bringing in their own manager." Sarah's laugh was rueful, and her small chin pointed downward as she added, "One more dead end. And damn, it would have been perfect for me."

The next step, Jonathan dimly imagined, would be a party or dinner of some sort at the McElroys', which he could not help mildly dreading, as he remembered the film critic's party, at which not only was almost everyone else gay (that would have been all right, except that some of the women did seem very hostile, to him) but they all smoked—heavily, some of them pipes and cigars—in three tiny rooms on Horatio Street.

However, it was they who were to entertain the McElroys at dinner, Sarah told him. "And I think just the four of us," she added. "That way it's easier, and I can make something great. And besides, who else?"

All true: an imaginative but fluky cook, Sarah did best on a small scale. And, too, the only other people they knew were fellow-transferees, as displaced and possibly as lonely as themselves, but otherwise not especially sympathetic.

The first surprise about Hattie McElroy, that first April night, was her size: she was a very big woman, with wild bleached straw-looking hair and round doll-blue eyes, and about twenty years older than Jonathan would have imagined; Sarah spoke of her as of a contemporary. Hugh McElroy was tall and gray and somewhat dim.

And Hattie was a very funny woman. Over drinks, she started right in with a description of a party she had been to the night before. "I was wearing this perfectly all-right dress, even if it was a tad on the oldish side," Hattie told them, as she sipped at her gin. "And Popsie Hooker—Can you imagine a woman my age, and still called Popsie? We went to Sunday school together, and she hasn't changed one bit. Anyway, Popsie said to me, 'Oh, I just love that dress you're wearing. I was so sorry when they went out of style five years ago.' Can you imagine? Isn't she marvellous? I just love Popsie, I truly do."

For such a big woman, Hattie's laugh was small, a little-girl laugh, but Jonathan found himself drawn to her big friendly teeth, her crazy hair.

Sarah, it then turned out, had met Popsie Hooker; early on in their stay in Hilton she had gone to a luncheon that Popsie gave for the new corporation wives. And, Sarah told Hattie, "She made a little speech that I didn't quite understand. About how she knew we were all very busy, so please not to write any thank-you notes. It was odd, I thought."

Hattie's chuckle increased in volume. "Oh, you don't understand Southern talk, not at all! I can tell you don't. That meant you were all supposed to write notes, and say you just couldn't resist writing, even if she said not to, since her lunch party was just so lovely."

Sarah laughed, too. "Well, dumb me. I took her at her word, and didn't write."

"Well, honey, you'll larn. But I can tell you, it takes near 'bout a lifetime."

Dinner was not one of Sarah's more successful efforts: veal Orloff, one of her specialties, but this time a little burned.

Hattie, though, seemed to think it was wonderful. "Oh, the trouble you must have gone to! And you must have a way with your butcher. I've just never seen veal like this—not down here."

Jonathan felt that she was overdoing it, but then chided himself: Hattie was Southern, after all; that was how they talked. He must not be negative.

"These mushrooms are truly delicious," Hugh McElroy put in. In Jonathan's view, a truer remark. Hugh was a kind and quiet man, who reminded Jonathan of someone; in an instant, to his mild surprise, he realized that it was his own father, whose shy manner had been rather like Hugh's.

A good evening, then. Jonathan could honestly say to Sarah that he liked her new best friends; they could even laugh over a few of the former candidates for that title.

Their return invitation, to a party at the McElroys', was less fun all around: too many people, in a cluttered but surprisingly formal house, on a too hot night in May. But by then it was almost time for the McElroys to leave, and Hattie had explained to Sarah that they just had to have all those people.

"They're really so loved around here," Sarah somewhat tipsily remarked, as they drove home from that party. "It just won't be the same town."

"It's still very pretty," Jonathan reminded her. "Smell the flowers."

The spring that had finally arrived, after so much rain, had seemed a reward for patience, with its extraordinary gifts of roses, azaleas, even gardenias, everywhere blooming, wafting sweetness into the light night air. And out in the woods white lacings of dogwood had appeared.

For some reason ("I can't think why! I must be going plumb crazy!" Hattie had confided to Sarah), Hattie and Hugh had agreed to be photographed over local TV on the day of their departure, and that night, on a news program, there they were: big Hattie, in her navy linen travelling suit, her white teeth all revealed in a grin for the camera, as she clutched an overflowing tote bag and tried to pin on a cluster of pink camellias; and tall Hugh, a shy smile as he waved an envelope of airline tickets.

As, watching, Sarah, who never cried, burst into tears.

And then they were gone, the McElroys. Moved out to New Mexico.

Sarah moped around. Indifferent housekeeping, minimal efforts. She made thrifty, ordinary meals, so unlike her usual adventurous, rather splashy culinary style, and she lost all interest in how she looked. Not that she was ever given to extravagance in those matters, but she used to wash and brush her hair a lot, and she did something to her eyes, some color, that Jonathan now recognized as missing, gone.

She often wrote to the McElroys, and Hattie answered, often; Sarah produced the letters for Jonathan to read at dinner. They contained a lot about the scenery, the desert, and fairly amusing gossip about what Hattie referred to as the Locals. "You would not believe the number of painters here, and the galleries. Seems like there's an opening most every night, and the Local Folk all come out in their fancy silver jewelry and their great big silver belts. Whole lots of the men are fairies, of course, but I just don't care. They're a lot of fun, they are indeed gay people." Funny, longish letters, with the sound of Hattie's voice, always ending with strong protestations of love and friendship. "Oh, we love you and miss you so much, the both of us!" cried out Hattie, on her thin flowered writing paper.

Jonathan observed all this with dark and ragged emotions —Sarah's deep sadness and the occasional cheer that Hattie's letters brought. He cared about Sarah in a permanent and complex way that made her pain his; still, what looked like true mourning for the absent McElroys gave him further pain. He had to wonder: was he jealous of the McElroys? And he had to concede that he was, in a way. He thought, I am not enough for her, and at the same time he recognized the foolishness of that thought. No one is "enough" for anyone, of course not. What Sarah needs is a job, and more friends that she likes; he knew that perfectly well.

And then one night at dinner, near the first of August, came the phone call from Hattie; Jonathan overheard a lot of exclamations and shouts, gasps from Sarah, who came back to the table all breathless, flushed.

"They're here! The McElroys are back, and staying at the Inn. Just for a visit. One of their boys suddenly decided to marry his girlfriend. Isn't that great?"

Well, it turned out not to be great. There was the dinner at Jonathan and Sarah's house, to which the McElroys came late, from another party (and not hungry; one of Sarah's most successful efforts wasted), and they left rather early. "You would not believe the day we have ahead of us tomorrow! And we thought marrying off a son was supposed to be easy." And the luncheon at Popsie Hooker's.

Jonathan and Sarah were not invited to the wedding, a fact initially excused (maybe overexcused) by Sarah: "We're not the Old Guard, not old Hiltonians, and besides, it's the bride's list, not Hattie's, and we don't even know her, or her family."

And then two weeks of the McElroy visit had passed, accurately calculated by Jonathan. Which calculation led to his fatal remarks, over all that wine, about the priorities of the McElroys.

On the morning after that terrible evening, Jonathan and Sarah have breakfast together as usual, but rather sombrely. Hung over, sipping at tea, nibbling at overripe late-summer fruit, Jonathan wonders what he can say, since he cannot exactly deny the truth of his unfortunate words.

At last he brings out "I'm really sorry I said that, about Hattie and Hugh."

Sarah gives him an opaque, level look, and her voice is judicious as she says, "Well, I'm sure you were right."

One of the qualities that Jonathan has always found exciting in Sarah is her ability to surprise him; she rarely behaves in ways that he would have predicted. Nevertheless, having worried intermittently during the day over her sadness, her low spirits and his own recent part in further lowering them, he is delighted (ah, his old astonishing Sarah) to find her all brushed and bright-eyed, happy, when he comes in the door that night.

"Well, I decided that all this moping around like an abandoned person was really silly," she tells him, over cold before-dinner glasses of wine, in the bright hot flower-scented dusk. "And so I just called Hattie, not being accusatory or anything. I just said that I'd really missed seeing her—them."

"Well, *great*." Jonathan is thinking how he admires her; she is fundamentally honest, and brave. And so pretty tonight, her delicately pointed face, her lively brown hair.

"Hattie couldn't have been nicer. She said they'd missed us, of course, but they just got so caught up in this wedding business. It's next Saturday—I'd lost track. They truly haven't had one minute, she told me, and I can believe her. Anyway, they're coming for supper on Sunday night. She said a post-wedding collapse would be just the best thing they could possibly think of."

"Well, great," Jonathan repeats, although some dim, indefinable misgiving has edged into his mind. How can one evening of friends at dinner be as terrific as this one will have to be? That question, after moments, emerges, and with it a darker, more sinister one: suppose it isn't terrific at all, as the last one was not?

By mid-August, in Hilton, it has been hot for so long that almost all the flowers have wilted, despite an occasional thundershower. Many people are away at that time, and in neglected gardens overblown roses shed fat satin petals onto drying, yellowing grass; in forgotten orchards sweet unpicked fruit falls and spatters, fermenting, slowly rotting, among tall summer weeds, in the simmering heat.

The Saturday of the McElroy son's wedding, however, is surprisingly cool, with an almost New England briskness in the air. That familiar-feeling air gives Jonathan an irrational flutter of hope: maybe the next night, Sunday, will be a reasonable evening. With the sort of substantive conversation that he and Sarah are used to, instead of some nutty Southern doubletalk. With this hope, the thought comes to Jonathan that Hattie imitating Popsie Hooker is really Hattie speaking her own true language. Dare he voice this to Sarah, this interesting perception about the nature of mimicry? Probably not.

Sarah spends a lot of Saturday cooking, so that it can all be served cold on Sunday night; she makes several pretty vegetable aspics, and a cold marinated beef salad. Frozen lemon soufflé. By Saturday night she is tired, but she and Jonathan have a pleasant, quiet dinner together. He has helped her on and off during the day, cutting up various things, and it is he who makes their dinner: his one specialty, grilled chicken.

Their mood is more peaceful, more affectionate with each other than it has been for months, Jonathan observes (since before they came down here? quite possibly).

Outside, in the gathering, lowering dusk, the just perceptibly earlier twilight, fireflies glimmer dimly from the pinewoods. The breeze is just barely cooler than most of their evening breezes, reminding Jonathan of the approach of fall—in his view, always a season of hope, of bright leaves on college campuses, and new courses offered.

.   .   .

Having worked so much the day before, Sarah and Jonathan have a richly indolent morning; they laze about. Around noon the phone rings, and Sarah goes to answer it. Jonathan, nearby, hears her say, "Oh, Hattie. Hi."

A very long pause, and then Sarah's voice, now stiff, all tightened up: "Well, no, I don't see that as a good idea. We really don't know Popsie—"

Another long pause, as Sarah listens to whatever Hattie is saying, and then, "Of course I understand, I really do. But I just don't think that Jonathan and I—"

A shorter pause, before Sarah says again, "Of course I understand. I do. Well, sure. Give us a call. Well, bye."

As she comes out to where Jonathan stands, waiting for her, Sarah's face is very white, except for her pink-tipped nose—too pink. She says, "One more thing that Hattie, quote, couldn't get out of. A big post-wedding do at Popsie Hooker's. She said of course she knew I'd been working my head off over dinner for them, so why didn't we just put it all in a basket and bring it on over there. They'd come and help." Unconsciously, perhaps, Sarah has perfectly imitated Hattie's inflections—even a few prolonged vowels; the effect is of a devastating irony, at which Jonathan does not smile.

"Jesus" is all he says, staring at Sarah, at her glistening, darkening eyes, as he wonders what he can do.

Sarah rubs one hand across her face, very slowly. She says, "I'm so tired. I think I'll take a nap."

"Good idea. Uh, how about going out to dinner?"

"Well, why not?" Her voice is absolutely level, controlled.

"I'll put some things away," Jonathan offers.

"Oh, good."

In the too small, crowded kitchen, Jonathan neatly packages the food they were to have eaten in freezer paper; he seals up and labels it all. He hesitates at marking the date, such an unhappy reminder, but then he simply writes down

the neutral numbers: 8, 19. By the time they get around to
these particular packages they will not attach any significance
to that date, he thinks (he hopes).

He considers a nap for himself; he, too, is tired, suddenly,
but he decides on a walk instead.

The still, hot, scrubby pinewoods beyond their house are now
a familiar place to Jonathan; he walks through the plumy,
triumphant weeds, the Queen Anne's lace and luxuriant
broomstraw, over crumbling, dry red clay. In the golden
August sunlight, he considers what he has always recognized
(or perhaps simply imagined that he saw) as a particular
look of Sundays, in terms of weather. Even if somehow he
did not know that it was Sunday, he believes, he could see
that it was, in the motes of sunlight. Here, now, today, the
light and the stillness have the same qualities of light and
stillness as in long-past Sundays in the Boston suburb where
he grew up.

Obviously, he next thinks, they will have to leave this
place, he and Sarah; it is not working out for them here, nothing is. They will have to go back to New York, look around,
resettle. And to his surprise he feels a sort of regret at the
thought of leaving this land, all this red clay that he would
have said he hated.

Immersed in these and further, more abstract considerations (old mathematical formulas for comfort, and less comforting thoughts about the future of the earth), Jonathan
walks for considerably longer than he intended.

Hurrying, as he approaches the house (which already
needs new paint, he distractedly notes), Jonathan does not at
all know what to expect: Sarah still sleeping (or weeping)
in bed? Sarah (unaccountably, horribly) gone?

What he does find, though, on opening the front door, is
the living room visibly pulled together, all tidied up: a tray

with a small bowl of ice, some salted almonds in another bowl, on the coffee table. And Sarah, prettily dressed, who smiles as she comes toward him. She is carrying a bottle of chilled white wine.

Jonathan first thinks, Oh, the McElroys must have changed their minds, they're coming. But then he sees that next to the ice bowl are two, and only two, glasses.

In a friendly, familiar way he and Sarah kiss, and she asks, "How was your walk?"

"It was good. I liked it. A real Sunday walk."

Later on, he will tell her what he thought about their moving away—and as Jonathan phrases that announcement he considers how odd it is for him to think of New York as "away."

Over their first glass of wine they talk in a neutral but slightly stilted way, the way of people who are postponing an urgent subject; the absence of the McElroys, their broken plans, trivializes any other topic.

At some point, in part to gain time, Jonathan asks her, "Have I seen that dress before?" (He is aware of the "husbandliness" of the question; classically, *they* don't notice.)

Sarah smiles. "Well, actually not. I bought it a couple of months ago. I just haven't worn it." And then, with a recognizable shift in tone, and a tightening of her voice, she plunges in. "Remember that night when you were talking about the McElroys? When you said we weren't so high on their priority list?"

Well, Jesus, of course he remembers, in detail; but Jonathan only says, very flatly, "Yes."

"Well, it's interesting. Of course I've been thinking about them all day, off and on. And what you said. And oh dear, how right you were. I mean, I knew you were *right*—that was partly what I objected to." Saying this, Sarah raises her face in a full look at him, acknowledging past pain.

What can he say? He is quiet, waiting, as she continues.

"But it's interesting, how you put it," she tells him. "How accurately. Prophetic, really. A lot of talk, and those letters! All about wonderful us, how great we are. But when you come right down to it—"

"The bottom line is old friends," Jonathan contributes, tentatively.

Pleased with him, Sarah laughs, or nearly; the sound she makes is closer to a small cough. But "Exactly," she says. "They poke a lot of fun at Popsie Hooker, but the reality is, that's where they are."

He tries again. "Friendships with outsiders don't really count? Does that cut out all Yankees, really?" He is thinking, Maybe we don't have to leave, after all? Maybe Sarah was just settling in? Eventually she will be all right here?

Grasping at only his stated question, about Yankees, Sarah gleefully answers, "Oh, very likely!" and she does laugh. "Because Yankees might do, oh, almost anything at all. You just can't trust a one of them."

As she laughs again, as she looks at Jonathan, he recognizes some obscure and nameless danger in the enthusiastic glitter of her eyes, and he has then the quite irrational thought that she is looking at him as though he were her new best friend.

However, he is able quickly to dismiss that flashed perception, in the happiness of having his old bright strong Sarah restored to him, their old mutually appreciative dialogue continuing.

He asks her, "Well, time to go out to dinner?"

"Oh yes! Let's go," she says, quickly getting to her feet.

Time in Santa Fe

It is midafternoon, on a brilliant August day, and I am sitting in a darkened bar, here in Santa Fe. I am drinking white wine with Jeffrey, an old friend who at any moment is going to tell me about his new gay life. I do not especially look forward to hearing his story; nothing against gayness, it is just that I have problems of my own that seem to make me selfish, a poor listener—although, being very fond of Jeffrey, I plan to make an effort.

We have a window table, and at this odd hour there is no one in the bar but us and the lanky, bored bartender, who is almost invisible, behind the bar, in the shadowy depths of the room. We can look out across Santa Fe's central square, the Plaza, where some Indians ("native craftsmen") have set up tables of brass jewelry, dazzling, flashing white gold, in the violently pure sunlight. On the other side of the Plaza more native craftspersons sit or squat behind their wares, over there mostly silver and turquoise. They are sheltered by the wide, outspread tiled eaves of an ancient Spanish building. And, spreading over everything is the extraordinary, vast Southwestern sky, its white clouds massed into sculptured monuments, incredibly slow-moving, and immense.

Neither Jeffrey nor I is much of a drinker, really; this bar simply seemed the only plausible thing for us to do next. In the morning, after my plane came in to Albuquerque, where Jeff met me and drove me up here, we walked up the Canyon Road; we "did" a lot of galleries there, and shops. We saw nearly the same paintings, same jewelry and rugs and embroidered clothing over and over again, repeated everywhere, until we both felt choked with the sight of so much merchandise. (We are neither of us buyers, or shoppers, really; even rich, or richer, we probably would not be.) We had an early lunch in a place where you have to stand in line, but that was nice, standing in the warm noon sunshine, in a patio of flowers; and for lunch we had something made with blue tortillas—I could hardly believe it, a rich dark blue, blue flour, Jeff said, and delicious.

Then we walked around the Plaza for a while, looking into more stores, but the pause for lunch had not renewed our interest in things for sale, and the day had begun to seem very, very hot. And so, when Jeffrey said, "Well, how about a nice cold glass of wine?" I said, "Great, great idea." We both knew that sooner or later we would have to talk about things, to say how we both were, and maybe some wine would help.

Jeffrey has had the same thick soft brown beard for the fifteen years that we have known each other (we first met in Berkeley, as students; I was just married then, and very pregnant) but when we were outside, in that merciless bright unimpeded sunlight, I could see some gray threads in the dark of his beard, and a few in his hair, which he still wears almost as long as he did in those old days. At that time Jeffrey was having a relationship (we all assumed) with a friend of his, David; but then, a few years later, he married Susan, a lawyer, blonde and good-looking (sort of). Now, having split from Susan, the new assumption is that he is gay again (David lives here too) and that he has come to Santa Fe to be gay, as well as to paint. So far, we have only talked very casually about mutual friends; I notice that we have not discussed either Susan or my husband, Rick. And, come to think of it, we have barely mentioned David; Jeffrey has only said that he is not here, he is visiting his mother in La Jolla.

I have just been visiting my own mother in Austin, Texas; this side trip to see Jeffrey before going home to Petaluma is an indulgence, but not much of one: juggling new airfares, going home an odd route through Denver, it only cost twenty dollars more than not stopping at all would have. Anyway, my mother has become an alcoholic, and a recluse, almost. She sits there all day, sipping sherry and smoking and watching soaps on TV, like someone a great deal older than she actually is. And she looks much older, too; she is both puffy and withered, at barely sixty. I don't know what to do about her.

Another problem on my mind is Rick. He is a building contractor; that seemed an eminently sensible move, from skilled carpenter to contractor, ten years ago, in the financially optimistic early seventies. But now he is out of work, and he is enraged—at everything in the world, me included. I have a teaching job, fourth grade, and so we are not as badly off as many people, but Rick keeps saying that I could be laid off too, which is true, of course, but I think in a way he hates it that I am the one still working, and it makes him hate me, a lot of the time.

And, more worries: Barbara, our daughter, who is only fifteen, wants to marry her boyfriend, Brad, who is all of eighteen (it is very possible that she either is or thinks she is pregnant).

And (this is sad) : our old cat, Puss, who is almost fifteen, a sort of wedding present, has almost stopped eating.

For some reason Puss is the one I think about the most. I don't know why. It is true that I love her very much; she is such an outrageous calico, with a bright orange patch on one eye, and a yellow stomach. We have been through a lot together, as it were. But I love those people too, my mother and Rick and Barbara, all of them, very much. Maybe in a way it is easier to think about Puss? And of course she is the only one who does not talk back; when, in my mind, I tell my mother to drink less, and tell Barbara not to get married and Rick not to be so angry, they all have a lot to say to me, in return (and this goes on all day, like a radio that I can't turn off).

I suddenly remember that Jeffrey has always had cats, and so I ask him, "Do you have a cat now, down here?"

He smiles, one faithful cat lover to another, and he says, "Of course. Actually we have three, a mother and two sons. The kittens were so cute we couldn't give them up. You know how that goes."

The "we" must mean David, whom of course I should ask about, but I am not quite ready for that. Easier to go on about cats. I tell him that I am a little worried about Puss, her not eating.

And Jeffrey remembers Puss—how endearing of him! "A really great cat," he proclaims, as I beam. And he goes on, "Who could forget an orange eye patch like that?" He tells me not to worry too much about her non-eating. Sometimes an older cat will just be off her feed for a while, he says, the way people sometimes are. He also says that he has a friend here in town with a beautiful calico cat who is *twenty-one years old.*

This is the best news I've heard in months, a cat that old. It is so good it makes me laugh. "Wow, twenty-one. I'll tell Puss she has to make it that far."

Jeffrey laughs too. "Well, sure she will."

However, my plane to Denver is not until ten tonight, and

we can't talk about cats all that time, although in a way I would like to.

And so, in a plunging-in way I ask him, "Well, how's David?"

Deliberately Jeffrey takes a drink of his wine, before he says, "Well, actually not too good. He had an operation, one of those real uglies. You know, they say they got everything? But you're so damaged. David is so damaged, I mean. That's what this trip to see his mother is all about. We don't know what to expect, really. Or when."

"Oh, Jeffrey." I reach across the table and take his hands, remembering as I do so, as I touch them, what beautiful long hands Jeffrey has. Holding hands for a moment we just look at each other—nothing else to do. I say, "I'm really sorry."

"Well, you're nice, but don't be sorry. We'll manage. And right now he's really okay. We're just sort of playing it by ear, day to day." As we both retrieve our hands, he adds, "He'll be sorry he didn't see you, of course. He sends love."

"Oh! Please give him my love."

We sit there quietly for several minutes, then, adjusting to the presence of this awful news of David, lying there between us like a stone.

Often, lately, as I castigate myself for such self-absorption in my own forms of trouble, I have thought about people in refugee camps, in the Middle East, or starving people anywhere, the hopeless, the genuinely anguished population of the world. But here is Jeffrey, directly in front of me, and while his troubles are nowhere near the horrible pains of those people, still his are considerably worse than mine, I think: a possibly (probably) dying loved person.

Like many shy people, Jeffrey tends to come out of silences into small speeches that have the sound of paragraphs. He always has (fifteen years is always); he does so now. "One thing I've meant to say to you," he says, into our silence, in the sun-moted room, "is that, uh, splitting with Susan had nothing to do with David. Although it could have looked like that. But she took off with a guy from art school. I felt pretty bad, and David said why not come down here. He was living with somebody at the time, and so the three of us shared a house for a while, which I have to say was not all that great." He gives me a twisting smile.

"I'll bet not," I tell him, trying to imagine how that would be: me and Rick and—and who?

"Anyway, then the other guy left, and there we were again, roommates. And then David got sick."

"*God,* Jeffrey."

"Yeah."

At that moment everything in our minds—in mine, for sure, and surely in Jeff's too—is so awful that as we look at each other across the table we begin to laugh, like nuts, or drunks (the bartender must think we've been drinking all day). We laugh and laugh, and when one of us stops the other starts off again. We exhaust ourselves.

"Oh God," he says, finally, wiping at his eyes with a big clean handkerchief. "Oh God, I'm so glad you came here to see me."

"Wait until I tell you all about my life," I say to him. "That'll really cheer you up." Which sets us off again, into minor hysterics.

Finally we sober up, so that I can tell him in an abbreviated way about my people, my concerns over them. He has never met my mother, and he only knew Barbara as a small child, and so it is Rick that I mostly talk about. "Basically he's just very depressed," I say. "And instead of cheering him up I get depressed too and that makes him feel worse. It's just so difficult, people living together, isn't it."

Jeffrey speaks slowly, and very thoughtfully. "Sometimes it does help, though," he says, "if you just accept the fact that you can't do a lot for anyone else. Then you stop trying so hard, and worrying over what feels like failure."

I consider this; it seems sensible, and even helpful. It is true that I can't do a lot for Rick, beyond being there, which sometimes he doesn't want. (Will he be more glad to see me after this trip? I have wondered.)

Jeffrey looks at his watch, just then, and I do too. It is much later than either of us imagined. We have talked for a long time. "I thought we'd have dinner here in town," Jeff says, "but now I wonder: maybe you'd rather come out to the house, and I'll rustle up a snack?"

"Oh, I'd really like that."

"I'd like you to see it." He smiles, adding, "And the cats." More soberly, a little anxiously, he further adds, "I really mean snack, though. With David gone I haven't been eating a lot. Like your Puss, I'm off my feed." Another smile.

"Well, I'd love to see your house. And the cats. And a snack would be great."

Once we have made this plan it seems so obviously what we should do that I wonder why Jeffrey didn't suggest it before; of course I would want to see his house and cats. And a tiny question flashes into my mind: could Jeffrey possibly have had some worry or shyness at the idea of our being alone, in an empty house, with David away at his mother's and Rick up in Petaluma? Just possibly he had, although there had never been a suggestion of that sort of feeling between us. Gayness aside, we are not each other's sexual types. Both being dark (we look just slightly alike, come to think of it: tall dark shy people who smile a lot), we both seem drawn to blond people. Rick is the blondest of all, big white-blond Swedish Rick, and David is blond, and so was—is

Susan. But you can't tell; sometimes men just think they are supposed to come on to you, at the oddest times. The oddest men.

We get out of the bar and we trod across the Plaza, past all the blindingly bright brass, and the Indians, to Jeffrey's car. His house is out on something called Bishop's Lodge Road, he tells me, maybe fifteen minutes out of town.

And, generous Jeff, he seems to have been thinking about my problems. (He has always been like that, I remember. Maybe that is a reason I came to see him?) Specifically, he has thought about my mother. "If she really doesn't care about her life, or looking good," he says, "if she just wants to anesthetize herself, I think you have to let her. What else can you do? Maybe this is the happiest she could be. I think you worry too much."

I can see that he is right, probably, and I am grateful—but at the moment it is hard for me to focus on my mother, in Austin; I am so overwhelmed by everything I see, the sand and rocks and sagebrush, the sheer stretch of space. Every shape, each color seems entirely new to me, and it is all so much larger and grander than anything, anywhere that I ever saw before.

Jeffrey's house is small, a white adobe shack, on a dirt road up off the highway—on a hill, with astounding views of further rocky, sandy hills, strange gray-green desert vegetation. We park and go into the house, and at first I think there is only one room, with a kitchen and long trestle table at one end. Some low couches, pillows, Indian rugs. But then I make out a sleeping loft. Still, hardly room for three people, David and his former lover, and Jeff—poor Jeff.

"Well, another glass of wine? We might as well?" Jeffrey begins to rummage about in the kitchen, and I see that I was right; having me here is making him nervous.

"Oh, it's so beautiful here," I tell him. "I really wish Rick could see it. And Barbara, actually, the dumb kid."

Happily, he seizes on this. "Well, why not?" in an eager way he asks me. "You could all come down? Even when David's back, we'd make do. You know, pretend it's fifteen years ago, and we're all sleeping around in bags."

We both laugh, and somehow the very idea of those absent people, my people, and his, has made Jeffrey easy with me again, and that silly bad moment is over.

The cats are something of a disappointment, though; scrawny and shy, they lack style, or maybe I've been spoiled by glamorous Puss. But I pat them and scratch their ears, and I tell Jeffrey that they are nice. What is actually nice is touching a cat at all. My mother is allergic to them, and so I had not had my hands on a cat for a week; it was like getting a fix.

All around us, on the walls, are big canvasses, filled with huge dim gray-green shapes, like mirrors of the desert. No way to tell whether the paintings are Jeffrey's or David's, and it doesn't seem right to ask. In any case, they are so much a part of the room, as well as of the landscape, that it feels unnecessary to remark on them at all.

For supper Jeffrey makes us omelets with sour cream and some greenish Mexican glop that I don't much like, but I appreciate his effort, of course. Most of all I appreciate the fact that my spirits have lightened, quite a lot; I really feel okay.

He makes very good coffee. It has the faintest taste of chocolate, and we talk some more, drinking coffee.

I'm worried over Rick, and my mother, and Barbara. And Puss. That is what, in effect, I say.

And Jeffrey says that he is worried and sad about David.

And we say to each other that we must not worry.

We are like people holding hands through a disaster, I think.

Later still, Jeffrey drives me down across the now-darkened desert to Albuquerque, to my plane, and on the way he tells me that he was serious about our visiting, all of us. "Or any one or two of you," he says, with a little laugh.

I tell him that it is a nice idea, nice of him, but in a practical way it seems very unlikely indeed, and I urge him to come up to see us, in Northern California.

However, as I settle into my seat on the plane, and buckle in, headed for Denver (which is certainly a long way to go, to get to Petaluma, California), then, along with a return of worry about what I am headed for, my same old problems, and my flying fears, I also experience a shot of warmth, of true comfort: there is Jeffrey, more or less permanently, in a place that I now have seen, and can visualize. Where I would always be welcome.

I smile to myself, in the dark, as I loftily imagine that I am speeding through fields of stars. I feel suddenly rich.

A Public Pool

Swimming

Reaching, pulling, gliding through the warm blue chlorinated water, I am strong and lithe: I am not oversized, not six feet tall, weighing one eighty-five. I am not myself, not Maxine. I am fleet, possessed of powerful, deep energy. I could swim all day, swim anywhere. Sometimes I even wonder if I should try the San Francisco Bay, that treacherous cold tide-wracked water. People do swim there, they call themselves Polar Bears. Maybe I should, although by now I like it here in the Rossi Pool, swimming back and forth, doing laps in the Fast Lane, stretching and pulling my forceful, invisible body.

Actually the lane where I swim is not really Fast. I swim during Recreational Swimming, and during Rec. hours what was Fast during Laps is roped off for anyone to use who does laps—Slow, Medium, or genuinely Fast, which I am not.

Last summer I started off in Slow, and then I could not do many lengths at a time, 16 or 18 at most, and only sidestroke. But I liked it, the swimming and the calm, rested way it seemed to make me feel. And I thought that maybe, eventually I might get thinner, swimming. Also, it takes up a certain amount of time, which for an out-of-work living-at-home person is a great advantage. I have been laid off twice in the past five years, both times by companies going out of business; I have a real knack, my mother says. And how many hours a day can a young woman read? That is a question my mother often asks. She is a downtown saleslady, old but blonde, and very thin.

So—swimming.

After a month or so I realized that I was swimming faster than most of the people in Slow, and that some people who could barely swim at all were in my way. For another two or three weeks I watched Medium, wondering if I dare try to swim in there. One day I forced myself, jumping into Medium, the middle lane. I felt very anxious, but that was hardly an unfamiliar or unusual sort of emotion; sometimes shopping for groceries can have the same effect. And actually Medium turned out to be okay. There were a few hotshots who probably belonged in Fast but were too chicken to try it there, but quite a few people swam about the same as I did, and some swam slower.

Sometime during the fall—still warm outside, big dry yellow sycamore leaves falling down to the sidewalks—the pool schedule changed so that all the lap swimming was geared to people with jobs: Laps at noon and after five. Discouraging: I knew that all those people would be eager, pushy aggressive swimmers, kicking big splashes into my face as they swam past, almost shoving me aside in their hurry to get back to their wonderful jobs.

However, I found out that during Rec. there is always a lane roped off for laps, and the Rec. hours looked much better: mid to late afternoon, and those can be sort of cold hours at home, a sad end of daytime, with nothing accomplished.

In any case, that is why I now swim my laps during Rec., in the Fast lane. In the rest of the pool some little kids cavort around, and some grownups, some quite fat, some hardly able to swim at all. Sometimes a lot of school kids, mostly girls, mostly black, or Asian. A reflection of this neighborhood, I guess.

To Meet Someone

Of course I did not begin swimming with any specific idea that I might meet someone, any more than meeting someone is in my mind when I go out to the Ninth Avenue Library. Still, there is always that possibility: the idea of someone is always there, in a way, wherever I go. Maybe everywhere everyone goes, even if most people don't think of it that way?

For one thing, the area of the Rossi Recreation Center, where the pool is, has certain romantic associations for me: a long time ago, in the sixties, when I was only in junior high (and still thin!), that was where all the peace marches started; everyone gathered there on the Rossi playing field, behind the pool house, with their placards and flags and banners, in their costumes or just plain clothes. I went to all the marches; I loved them, and I hated LBJ, and I knew that his war was crazy, wicked, killing off kids and poor people, mostly blacks, was how it looked to me. Anyway, one Saturday in May, I fell in with a group of kids from another school, and we spent the rest of that day together, just messing around, walking almost all over town—eating pizza in North Beach and smoking a little dope in the park. Sort of making out, that night, at one of their houses, over on Lincoln Way. Three guys and a couple of girls, all really nice. I kept hoping that I would run into them somewhere again, but I never did. Or else they, too, underwent sudden changes, the

way I did, and grew out-of-sight tall, and then fat. But I still
think of them sometimes, walking in the direction of Rossi.

Swimming, though: even if you met someone it would be
hard to tell anything about them, beyond the most obvious
physical facts. For one thing almost no one says anything,
except for a few superpolite people who say Sorry when they
bump into you, passing in a lane. Or, there is one really mean-
looking black woman, tall, and a very fast swimmer, who one
day told me, "You ought to get over closer to the side." She
ought to have been in Fast, is what I would like to have said,
but did not.

The men all swim very fast, and hard, except for a couple
of really fat ones; most men somersault backward at the end
of each length, so as not to waste any time. A few women
do that, too, including the big mean black one. There is one
especially objectionable guy, tall and blond (but not as tall
as I am), with a little blond beard; I used to watch him zip
past, ploughing the water with his violent crawl, in Fast,
when I was still pushing along in Medium. Unfortunately,
now he, too, comes to swim in Rec., and mostly at the same
times that I do. He swims so fast, so roughly cutting through
the water; he doesn't even know I am there, nor probably
anyone else. He is just the kind of guy who used to act as
though I was air, along the corridors at Washington High.

I have noticed that very few old people come to swim at
Rossi. And if they do you can watch them trying to hide their
old bodies, slipping down into the water. Maybe for that
reason, body shyness, they don't come back; the very old never
come more than once to swim, which is a great pity, I think.
The exercise would be really good for them, and personally
I like very old people, very much. For a while I had a job
in a home for old people, a rehabilitation center, so-called,
and although in many ways it was a terrible job, really ex-
hausting and sometimes very depressing, I got to like a lot of

them very much. They have a lot to say that's interesting, and if they like you it's more flattering, I think, since they have more people to compare you with. I like *real* old people, who look their age.

People seem to come and go, though, at Rossi. You can see someone there regularly for weeks, or months, and then suddenly never again, and you don't know what has happened to that person. They could have switched over to the regular lap hours, or maybe found a job so that now they come very late, or early in the morning. Or they could have died, had a heart attack, or been run down by some car. There is no way you could ever know, and their sudden absences can seem very mysterious, a little spooky.

Garlic for Lunch

Since my mother has to stay very thin to keep her job (she has to look much younger than she is), and since God knows I should lose some weight, we usually don't eat much for dinner. Also, most of my mother's money goes for all the clothes she has to have for work, not to mention the rent and the horrible utility bills. We eat a lot of eggs.

However, sometimes I get a powerful craving for something really good, like a pizza, or some pasta, my favorite. I like just plain spaghetti, with scallions and garlic and butter and some Parmesan, mostly stuff we have already in the house. Which makes it all the harder not to yield to that violent urge for pasta, occasionally.

One night there was nothing much else around to eat, and so I gave in to my lust, so to speak. I made a big steaming bowl of oniony, garlicky, buttery spaghetti, which my mother, in a worse than usual mood, ate very little of. Which meant that the next day there was a lot left over, and at noontime, I was unable not to eat quite a lot of it for lunch. I brushed my teeth before I went off to swim, but of course that doesn't help a lot, with garlic. However, since I almost never talk to anyone at Rossi it didn't much matter, I thought.

I have worked out how to spend the least possible time undressed in the locker room: I put my bathing suit on at home, then sweatshirt and jeans, and I bring along under-things wrapped up in a towel. That way I just zip off my clothes to swim, and afterward I can rush back into them, only naked for an instant; no one has to see me. While I am swimming I leave the towel with the understuff wrapped up in it on the long bench at one side of the pool, and some-times I have horrible fantasies of someone walking off with it; however, it is comforting to think that no one would know whose it was, probably.

I don't think very much while swimming, not about my old bra and panties, nor about the fact that I ate all that garlic for lunch. I swim fast and freely, going up to the end with a crawl, back to Shallow with my backstroke, reaching wide, stretching everything.

Tired, momentarily winded, I pause in Shallow, still crouched down in the water and ready to go, but resting.

Just then, startlingly, someone speaks to me, a man's con-versational voice. "It's nice today," he says. "Not too many people, right?"

Standing up, I see that I am next to the blond-bearded man, the violent swimmer. Who has spoken.

Very surprised, I say, "Oh yes, it's really terrific, isn't it. Monday it was awful, so many people I could hardly move, really terrible. I hate it when it's crowded like that, hardly worth coming at all on those days, but how can you tell until you get here?" I could hear myself saying all that; I couldn't stop.

He looks up at me in—amazement? disgust? great fear,

that I will say even more. It is hard to read the expression in his small blue bloodshot eyes, and he only mutters, "That's right," before plunging back into the water.

Was it my garlic breath or simply my height, my incredible *size* that drove him off like that? In a heavy way I wondered, as I continued to swim, all the rest of my laps, which seemed laborious. It could have been either, easily, or in fact anything about me could have turned him off, off and away, for good; I knew that he would never speak to me again. A pain which is close to and no doubt akin to lust lay heavily in my body's lower quadrant, hurtful and implacable.

Sex

The atmosphere in the pool is not exactly sexy, generally, although you might think that it would be, with everyone so stripped down, wearing next to nothing, and some of the women looking really great, so slim and trim, high-breasted, in their thin brief bathing suits.

Once, just as I was getting in I overheard what looked like the start of a romance between a young man, fairly good-looking, who was talking to a very pretty Mexican girl.

The girl said, "You're Brad?"

"No. Gregory."

"Well, Greg, I'll try to make it. Later."

But with brief smiles they then both plunged back into doing their laps, seeming not to have made any significant (sexual) contact.

I have concluded that swimming is not a very sexual activity. I think very infrequently of sex while actually swimming. Well, all sports are supposed to take your mind off sex, aren't they? They are supposed to make you miss it less?

The lifeguards, during swimming hours, usually just sit

up on their high wooden lifeguard chairs, looking bored. A couple of youngish, not very attractive guys. Every now and then one of the guys will walk around the pool very slowly, probably just to break his own monotony, but trying to look like a person on patrol.

One afternoon I watched one of those guys stop at Shallow, and stare down for a long time at a little red-haired girl who was swimming there. She was a beautiful child, with narrow blue eyes and long wet red hair, a white little body, as lithe as a fish, as she laughed and slipped around. The lifeguard stared and stared, and I knew—I could tell that sex was on his mind. Could he be a potential child molester?

I myself think of sex more often, in spite of swimming, since the day Blond Beard spoke to me, the day I'd had all that garlic for lunch. I hate to admit this.

The Shrink

An interesting fact that I have gradually noticed as I come to Rossi, to swim my laps, is that actually there is more variety among the men's trunks than among the bathing suits the women wear. The men's range from cheap, too-tight Lastex to the khaki shorts with thin blue side stripes that they advertise at Brooks, or Robert Kirk. Whereas, as I noted early on, all the women wear quite similar-looking dark suits. Do the men who are rich, or at least getting along okay in the world, not bother to hide it when they come to a cheap public pool, while the women do? A puzzle. I cannot quite work it out. Blond Beard wears new navy Lastex trunks, which might mean anything at all.

Most people, including a lot of the men, but not Blond Beard, wear bathing caps, which makes it even harder to tell people apart, and would make it almost impossible, even, to recognize someone you knew. It is not surprising that from time to time I see someone I think I know, or have just met somewhere or other. At first, remembering the peace march kids, I imagined that I saw one or all of them, but that could have been just hope, a wishful thought. I thought I saw my old gym teacher, also from junior-high days. And one day I saw a man who looked like my father, which was a little crazy, since he split for Seattle when I was about five years old; I probably wouldn't know him if I did see him somewhere, much less in a pool with a bathing cap on.

But one day I saw an old woman with short white hair, swimming very fast, whom I really thought was the shrink I went to once in high school, as a joke.

Or, going to the shrink started out to be a joke. The school had a list of ones that you could go to, if you had really "serious problems," and to me and my girlfriend, then, Betty, who was black, it seemed such a ludicrous idea, paying another person just to listen, telling them about your sex life, all like that, that we dreamed up the idea of inventing some really serious problems, and going off to some fool doctor and really putting him on, and at the same time finding out what it was like, seeing shrinks.

Betty, who was in most ways a lot smarter than me, much faster to catch on to things, chickened out early on; but she kept saying that I should go; Betty would just help me make up some stuff to say. And we did; we spent some hilarious afternoons at Betty's place in the project, making up lists of "serious problems": heavy drugs, of course, and dealers. And stepfathers or even fathers doing bad sex things to you, and boys trying to get you to trick. All those things were all around Betty's life, and I think they scared her, really, but she laughed along with me, turning it into one big joke between us.

I made the appointment through the guidance office, with

a Dr. Sheinbaum, and I went to the address, on Steiner Street. And that is where the joke stopped being a joke.

A nice-looking white-haired lady (a surprise right there; I had expected some man) led me into a really nice-looking living room, all books and pictures and big soft comfortable leather furniture. And the lady, the doctor, asked me to sit down, to try to tell her about some of the things that upset me.

I sat down in a soft pale-colored chair, and all of the funny made-up stuff went totally out of my mind—and I burst into tears. It was horrible, great wracking sobs that I absolutely could not stop. Every now and then I would look up at the doctor, and see that gentle face, that intelligent look of caring, and for some reason that made me cry much harder, even.

Of course I did not tell Betty—or anyone—about crying like that. All I said about going to the shrink was that it was all right, no big deal. And I said about the good-looking furniture. Betty was interested in things like that.

But could the fast-swimming older woman be that shrink? Well, she could be; it seemed the kind of thing that she might do, not caring what anyone thought, or who might see her. But she would never remember or recognize me—or would she?

Looking for Work

The job search is something that I try not to think about, along with sex, general deprivation. It is what I should be doing, naturally; and in theory that is what I do all day, look for work. However, these days I seldom get much further than the want ads in the paper, those columns and columns of people saying they want secretaries, or sales people. And no one, not in a million years, would think of hiring me for either of those slots. Secretaries are all about the same size, very trim and tidy-looking, very normal, and so are people in sales—just ask my mother.

Sometimes an ad for a waitress sounds possible, and that is something I've done; I had a part-time waitress job the summer I got out of Washington High. But in those days I was thinner, and just now my confidence is pretty low. In my imagination, prospective employers, restaurant owners take one look at me and they start to sneer: "We don't even have the space for a person your size," or some such snub.

Instead I swim, and swim, swim—for as long as I can, every day. I can feel my muscles stretching, pulling, getting longer, in the warm strong water.

Hello

An odd coincidence: on a Tuesday afternoon—short Rec. hours, one-thirty to three—both Blond Beard *and* the big black woman who told me to swim closer to the side, so crossly—both those people on that same day said Hello to me, very pleasantly.

First, I had just jumped down into the pool, the shallow end of the lap section, when Blond Beard swam up and stood beside me for a minute. Looking up at me, he said Hello, and he smiled. However, his small pale eyes were vague; very likely he did not remember that we sort of talked before (hopefully, he did not remember the garlic).

I concentrated on not making too much of that encounter.

Later, when I had finished swimming and was drying off and dressing in the locker room, I was half aware that someone else was in there, too, on the other side of a row of lockers. Hurrying, not wanting to see anyone (or anyone to see me!), I was about to rush out of the room when at the exit door I almost bumped into the big black woman. In fact, it was a little funny, we are so nearly the exact same size. We both smiled; maybe she saw the humor in it, too? And then she said, "Say, your stroke's coming along real good."

"Oh. Uh, thanks."

"You're a real speeder these days."

I felt a deep pleasure in my chest. It was like praise from a teacher, someone in charge. We walked out of the building together, the black woman going up across the playground, where the peace marches gathered, maybe toward Geary Boulevard. And I walked down Arguello, out into the avenues. Home.

Warmth

The water in the pool is warm. In our cold apartment, where my mother screams over the higher and higher utility bills and keeps the heat down, I only have to think about that receiving warmness, touching all my skin, to force myself out into the cold and rain, to walk the long blocks to Rossi Pool, where quickly undressed I will slip down into it.

And swim.

In January, though, the weather got suddenly warmer. The temperature in the pool also seemed to have suddenly changed; it was suddenly cooler. Distrustful, as I guess I tend to be regarding my perceptions, I wondered if the water only seemed cooler. Or, had they turned it down because of the warmer weather, economizing, as my mother does? In any case it was disappointing, and the pool was much less welcoming, no matter how falsely spring-like the outside air had turned.

"Do you think the water's colder?" It was Blond Beard who asked this of me one day; we were standing momen-

tarily in the shallow end. But although I was the person he
had chosen to ask, I was still sure that for him I was no one;
he remembers nothing of me from one tiny, minor contact
to another. I am a large non-person.

I told him, "Yes, it seems a little colder to me" (not wanting to say too much—again).

"They must have turned it down."

Swimming

Since the pool is 100 feet long, a half mile is 26 lengths,
which is what I try to do every day. "I swim three miles a
week," would sound terrific, to anyone, or even, "I swim a
little over two miles a week." Anyone would be impressed,
except my mother.

On some days, though, I have to trick myself into swimming the whole 26. "I'm tired, didn't sleep too well, 16
lengths is perfectly okay, respectable," I tell myself. And
then, having done the 16, I will say (to myself) that I might
as well do a couple more, or four more. And if you get to 20
you might as well go on to 26, as I almost always do.

On other, better days I can almost forget what I am
doing; that is, I forget to count. I am only aware of a long
strong body (mine) pulling through the water, of marvellous
muscles, a strong back, and long, long legs.

The Neighborhood

Sometimes, walking around the neighborhood, I see swimmers from the pool—or, people I think I have seen in swimming; in regular clothes it is hard to be sure.

Once, passing a restaurant out on Clement Street I was
almost sure that the waitress with her back to the window
was the big black woman, formerly cross but now friendly

and supportive. Of course I could go in and check it out, even say Hello, but I didn't want to do that, really. But I was pleased with just the idea that she might be there, with a waitress job in such a nice loose-seeming coffee place. I even reasoned that if they hired that woman, big as she is, mightn't someone hire me, about the same size? (I think swimming is making me more optimistic, somehow.) Maybe I should look harder, not be so shy about applying for waitress jobs?

However, one day in late June, there is no mistaking Blond Beard, who comes up to me on Arguello, near Clement: I am just coming out of the croissant place where I treated myself to a cup of hot chocolate. I am celebrating, in a way: the day before I had pulled all my courage together and went out to a new "rehabilitation place" for old people, out in the Sunset, and they really seemed to like me. I am almost hired, I think. They would give me a place to live— I could leave home!

"Hey! I know you from swimming, don't I? In Rossi?" Blond Beard has come up close to me; he is grinning confidently up into my face. His clothes are very sharp, all clean and new, like from a window at Sears.

"You look so good, all that swimming's really trimmed you down," he tells me. And then, "This is a coincidence, running into you like this when I was needing a cup of coffee. Come on back in and keep me company. My treat."

He is breathing hard up into my face, standing there in the soft new sunlight. I am overwhelmed by the smell of Juicy Fruit—so much, much worse than garlic, I suddenly decide. And I hate sharp clothes.

Stepping back I say, "Thanks, but I have to go home now," and I move as smoothly as though through water.

I leave him standing there.

I swim away.

Waiting for Stella

Actually it is Jimmy, Stella's fourth and final husband (Stella died a month ago), for whom everyone is waiting, all these old people, in this large sunny clearing in a grove of ancient redwoods. It is high noon, on a bright October day, and time for lunch, but Rachel, the hostess, has delayed serving the food, because of Jimmy's lateness. This will be everyone's first sight of him since Stella's death; he took off for Santa Barbara just afterward to visit a sister there, and presumably to recuperate, travelling in Stella's old car. Perhaps the car is making him late this morning? The guests, old friends, sip nervously at tomato juice or club soda, while a few of the hardier ones have white wine; they are all in their seventies or eighties, except for a young dark, vividly pretty girl, Day, a visiting friend of Rachel's, who will help with lunch.

Everyone, including Rachel and her husband, Baxter, and Day, the visiting girl, is seated at a long bandanna-cloth-covered table, on benches. Not far from the table is a small oval concrete swimming pool, its unused murky water now flat and still. Here and there in the grove are clumps of huge thick-fronded ferns, a dusty gray green, quite motionless, in the moted sunlight.

They are all waiting for Jimmy, of course, but it is Stella whose lively absence dominates the mood, so that several people, especially Rachel and Baxter, have to remind themselves that they are waiting for Jimmy, not for Stella.

Rachel and Baxter's house is up on a knoll, invisible from the pool, among tall thick eucalyptus trees, gray thickets of manzanita. It is a big house, though cheaply and somewhat flimsily constructed of clapboard, now nicely weathered to silver. It was a great bargain forty years ago when Rachel and her first husband had it built. Now it is probably worth a lot of money, as she and Baxter wryly say to each other from time to time, and they add, "but only if we sell it." (Baxter is Rachel's third husband, and surely her last, she thinks.) Near the house, a little way down toward the pool, is the guest cabin, slatted, green.

All the houses in this small enclave, in the Santa Cruz Mountains, are somewhat similar, as, not quite accidentally, are their owners; friends, they all were professional people, "liberals," mildly intellectual. Rachel was a doctor, a professor of medicine, rather distinguished; Baxter, although he inherited money, was an art critic. Stella was a painter.

What once were vacation homes now house their retirements.

In those younger, summer days, feelings sometimes ran high: dissensions occurred over love affairs, real or imagined; opposing political views split their ranks. But now old feuds are quieted, if not forgotten—especially today, as in an almost unified way they think about Stella, the first of them to die, and they think about Jimmy, who is *very* late.

Now, conferring with Day, Rachel decides to go ahead and serve the first course, a gazpacho, which has already been brought down and is sitting there on the table, in its huge green-glazed tureen. And so Rachel ladles out the soup, and Day takes the bowls around to everyone.

Actually, Stella has always been a sort of unifying principle for this group, in that they have generally been united in opposition to whatever she was doing. Not actual opposition to her views, but Stella always, somehow, went too far. Wonderful of her to march in Selma at already sixty-odd, but did she have to get arrested, so purposefully, and spend a week in that jail? Or, more recently, was it necessary, really, that she scale the fence at Diablo Canyon, protesting nuclear power? Not to mention the fact that she often drank too much, and almost always talked too much, with her proud white tooth-flashing grin; she had too many husbands and lovers (though fortunately, it was sometimes remarked, no children).

Her final marriage to Jimmy Scott, a former alcoholic, former film director (not important), was hard to understand, the other husbands having been, in their ways, almost predictable: Jack, a Communist, and Jewish (this was daring, in 1922, for a New England girl of "good"—Republican, Unitarian—family); Horace, a black longshoreman; and Yosh, a Japanese painter, whom she married just after Pearl Harbor (of course). But—Jimmy?

During the illness preceding Stella's death, however, the mercifully short three months, Jimmy's behavior toward her was observed to be exemplary. It was hardly a time when anyone would have behaved badly, but still his patience was remarkable. He searched for out-of-print books that Stella mentioned wanting to reread, for out-of-season flowers for her bedroom (they were not rich people, not at all), for special delicate foods, rare fruits to tempt her waning appetite.

In the last awful month of her life, although she stayed at

home, in the house up the road from Rachel and Baxter's, Stella refused (through Jimmy, of course) to let anyone visit her; not even Rachel, a doctor, was allowed to see her then, which no one quite understood, except, just possibly, Rachel.

Of the dozen people there—thirteen, counting Day—only Day is not thinking in a concentrated way about Stella. Day is thinking painfully, obsessively of Allen, the lover whom she came to California to see, but with whom things did not work out; they just broke up in San Francisco, where Allen lives. Scenes and quarrels, all terrible to recall. Passing breadsticks, Day considers the phrase "to break up." It is odd, she thinks, that people always say "break up *with*," since the whole point of breaking up is that you are no longer *with* but alone.

In order not to think about Allen, and then, too, because it seems appropriate, Day makes a conscious effort to think about Stella, whom she met fairly often, over the years, at Rachel's. (Day's mother, also a doctor, a friend of Rachel's, named Day for her heroine, Dorothy Day, who was also much admired by Rachel.) Stella was perfectly all right, Day thinks, but she talked so much. And that hair. Bright red hair, for a woman in her seventies or (probably) eighties? More generously, Day then admits to herself that you can't tell what you'll do that far ahead. She herself at eighty might dye her hair purple, or green, a one-person revival of punk, in the year two thousand and whatever, out of sheer boredom with living that long.

Stella never seemed bored with her old age—you had to give her that. And even if Jimmy bored her she never let it be known. ("Jimmy was actually more interesting as an alcoholic," Baxter has remarked. "Poor Stella! No luck at all with men.")

Day, who in her grief is not even aware of how pretty she is, now sits down with her own cold bowl of soup, next to Baxter, who must have been extremely handsome, a long time ago, Day imagines.

Baxter, who dislikes gazpacho (the peppers seem to disagree with him, or perhaps the cucumbers), looks for diversion at Day's long thin brown legs, now exposed beneath her loose flowered skirt, in high rope clogs. Day's legs, which Baxter much admires, lead him back to a sensual dream of Stella. He sees a room in the Sherry Netherland, in New York (he has just married Rachel; she is waiting for him, up in Connecticut—she is giving a seminar at Yale). Gold coverlets drawn back on sumptuous beds, in the half-light of an August afternoon. Champagne in a silver bucket, two chilled glasses. And Stella: all that pink-gold flesh (she was fairly plump in those days), all that flesh, half revealed, half concealed. Silk, rows of lace. That flesh, breasts, and that brilliant hair, spread on her pillow, his pillow.

But even in his dream he, Baxter, is actually sitting there alone, and fully dressed. And he never saw any flesh of Stella's beyond that revealed in a modest bathing suit. For Stella, if the truth were known, and he trusts that it is not— Stella had stood him up. There he was, expecting her, in that room, with champagne, and the next day she had the consummate gall to say, "But Baxter, darling, I can't believe you were serious." And that awful laugh. What a bitch, when you came right down to it—really surprising that more people didn't see through her. He wonders if Rachel did; he has never been sure just how Rachel felt about Stella. Well, there's no possibility of understanding women, as he has always said.

More crossly than he meant to, Baxter whispers to Day,

"Why do you think Rachel serves this damned soup so often?"

Startled, Day answers him literally. "She thinks it's good in hot weather, I guess." And then she says the next thing that enters her grief-dulled mind: "And it seems a more leftist sort of soup than vichyssoise."

Baxter emits a loud cackling laugh. "Oh, very good," he tells Day, who has not meant to be funny, especially. "A leftist soup. That's *very good.*"

Baxter's laugh and some words of this small exchange have caught everyone's attention, so that it all has to be re-peated several times, and explained, many of those old ears not being quite what they once were. No one seems to think "leftist soup" is quite as funny as Baxter did. (Rachel espe-cially, in the way of wives, did not find it awfully funny. Why did she marry Baxter, she wonders. But even if she knew, it is much too late to reconsider.) However, at least a diversion was created, from so many sad thoughts of Stella, and such anxiety as how to deal with Jimmy: how will he be?

This October day is unseasonably hot; everyone has agreed on that, and commented at length. Even in this shaded glen, where usually it is cool, often cold, almost always too cold for swimming in the dark greenish pool, today it is very warm, so that swimming is at least discussed. Warm shafts of light fall dustily between the redwoods, on the thick still tessellated fronds of ferns.

Stella, of course, would have been in hours ago, flopping around like a porpoise and exhorting everyone else to come in, too. No one has remarked on this probability, but what Stella would have been doing has occurred to everyone there. They will continue to think, in other contexts, of what Stella would have done.

However, the heat is actually a relief to so many old bones; they bask and relax in it. And the warm weather seems a reprieve of sorts, to these old people. The fact is that their location, in these mountains south of San Francisco, is not an ideal spot for the retired, for the very old. They are vulnerable to such extremes of cold, and to floods, from mountain streams, as well as to spectres of isolation, loneliness, helplessness. Danger. They have all thought and talked from time to time of moving somewhere else, but where? And for them to move would seem a sort of giving up, giving in, a yielding to old age and infirmity.

This day, though, is reassuring; they are still all right, exactly where they are.

And, as no one says, and perhaps no one is really aware, it is rather a relief not to have Stella around, loudly splashing in the pool, and always urging them all to exceed themselves, somehow.

Although they were very close friends, as far as anyone knew, and were almost exactly the same age, Rachel's and Stella's personal styles were very different. Rachel's low-key, toned-down quiet mode could almost have been developed in opposition to Stella's flamboyance. All three of Rachel's husbands, including Baxter, have affectionately compared her to a wren, a coincidence that tactful Rachel has mentioned to no one, surely not to Baxter, who despite his money and good looks is quite insecure.

Rachel is small, with neat gray-brown hair and finely lined lightly tanned skin. When Baxter came home to her that time in Connecticut, just mentioning that he had "caught a glimpse" of Stella in New York, Rachel quite accurately surmised what had happened: Baxter had made a pass, of some sort, and Stella in some way had turned him down. Curiously, at first she was a little annoyed at Stella: poor

Baxter, aging is hard on such a handsome man. But it soon came to her, causing a wry, inward smile, that after all if Stella had said yes, she, Rachel, would have been considerably more annoyed.

Standing just off from the group, near the end of the table, Day and Rachel now consult with each other, Rachel saying, "Well, I just don't know. Jimmy's usually so punctual," and she frowns.

"He might feel worse if we waited," Day offers. "Worse about everything, I mean."

Rachel gives Day an attentive, interested look. (Rachel listens to what other people say.) "Well, of course you're absolutely right," she says. "Besides, it's making everyone nervous. We'll just go ahead with the salmon."

"He might always call and say that he isn't coming after all," Day further contributes. She is thinking: Allen might call.

"Oh, right," says Rachel.

It is true that the prolonged absence of Jimmy is nervously felt, all around. People speculate about what could have happened. Flat tires are mentioned, as well as being out of gas, or lost. What no one voices is the fear, felt by almost all of them, that he could have started drinking again. Stella was believed to have helped get him off the bottle.

Someone, more mean-spirited than the rest, has just said, "I hope our dear Jimmy hasn't stopped off at some bar," when fortunately Rachel and Day arrive with their platters of cold salmon, the glistening silvery pink surrounded by various shades of green—parsley and several sauces—so that everyone can exclaim over the beauty of the food.

.   .   .

will go off with that fellow, that young Allen (well, off to bed). And that Baxter will take a nap, by himself.

All these things do take place, but not quite as anyone would have expected.

In bed, after a brief interval of love, Day and Allen take up their argument again.

Allen believes that they should marry. In a fast-disintegrating world, a personal commitment is almost all that is left, he thinks. Let us love one another or die, he says. Ah, love, let us be true. Besides, he is making a lot of money in San Francisco, in real estate.

Well, Day does not see marriage as an ultimate commitment. She does love Allen, and she is true. But still. And she has hopes of being accepted at law school, in New Haven.

Well, if she must, then why not Stanford, or Berkeley, or Davis?

In the waning late-afternoon light, the cool fall end of that golden October day, their words rise in the air, in circles and patterns that then, like smoke, dissolve, and Day and Allen fall asleep, in the high narrow guest bed, in the flimsily slatted green-stained cabin.

In the kitchen, clearing up, Rachel and Jimmy do not fall into a conversation having to do with Stella; they do not even mention Stella. Instead, they discuss Santa Barbara, and Jimmy's plans to go there, to live with his sister.

"It's a most charming place," he tells Rachel, as he polishes glasses (remembering that Stella thought they came out brighter with paper than with linen. "Such an affectation, linen towels," she used to say). "And the flowers," Jimmy now tells Rachel, quickly. Well, the flowers. And it's interesting, he continues, how some people seem to mellow with age: his sister, who for years was such a terror, now is very nice, a kind and pleasant person.

"I suppose that must be true," murmurs Rachel, who is wondering if either of those adjectives, kind and pleasant, would ever apply to Baxter, and if so, when.

"When I'm settled there, you've got to come and visit," Jimmy says.

Baxter goes off to bed, alone, of course, but despite the huge new down quilt and the lowered blinds and all the soothing books (his favorites, Ruskin and Swinburne, odd tastes, perhaps somewhat misleading, having to do with his mother), despite all the available comforts of the bedroom, poor Baxter is quite unable to sleep, even to doze for a minute or two.

He is thinking of Day and Allen, rancorously, uncontrollably. His are not exactly personal thoughts; he is simply thinking of youth, of obviously taken-for-granted health and sensuality. The condition of youth now seems to Baxter a club from which he has abruptly and most unfairly been excluded.

A couple of hours later Jimmy has gone. Outside, the night has turned black and cold, and a wind has come up, rattling leaves, shaking windowpanes, but Rachel remains in the small bright kitchen. Everything is clean and put away, and she is tired. She has made herself a small pot of tea, and she sits sipping, at the kitchen table. She thinks, How wonderful not to be talking to anyone, not even thinking of people.

However, this is not to last, as she might have known that it would not: light footsteps in the passageway hurry toward her, someone else with something to say, or ask.

And of course it is Day.

"Well," Day begins, with a smile of pure pleasure at the

sight of Rachel which almost dissolves Rachel's wish that she not be there. "Oh, I hoped I'd find you," says Day. "I slept for a while, and I had such an odd dream, about Stella. So vivid." She smiles again, disarmingly. "In the dream, I asked her point-blank how come she married Jimmy, and she told me, but what's terrible is that I can't remember what she said!"

"Would you like some tea? The cups are right there behind you."

Day sits down with her tea. In her old loose blue cotton robe, with her just-washed face, she looks even younger than she is. She says, "Well, it was really a nice lunch party?"

What was intended as a statement has come out as a question, at which Rachel smiles. "I guess," she says. "I wanted Jimmy to have a good time, and to feel that everyone liked him, after all. I wish that damned old car hadn't made him so late. On the other hand . . ."

She has left her thought dangling, but Day takes it up. "On the other hand, maybe just as well? Time enough?" she asks, in her clear young voice.

"Could be. Enough of all of us. We don't really make up for Stella." She adds, after the smallest pause, "And I thought Baxter was especially cross. Men are so much less forgiving than women are, don't you think?" She sighs, at this quite unintended afterthought.

"Oh really, how do you mean?"

Day is so eager that Rachel regrets her observation. "Well, maybe it's not even true."

But Day is relentless. "What does Baxter have against Jimmy, do you think?" she pursues.

"Well, basically just his marrying Stella. It was Stella that Baxter had it in for, so to speak."

Day asks, "Because of her politics, you mean?"

"Well, that among other things. Actually, a lot of men

didn't like her, not at all. It was odd, I always thought. Men are supposed to like beautiful women." Rachel's voice is reedy, low and rather tired, an old thrush.

"You mean, men fell in love with her but really didn't like her much?" Day's tone is that of someone zeroing in—perhaps a lawyer's tone.

Rachel smiles. With exhausted emphasis she says, "Exactly. That's just what Stella said, in fact. I think it made her lonely, a lot of the time."

"Especially since no one would see what was going on. Oh, I can see that," Day improvises.

"And Jimmy liked her very much, it's that simple," Rachel concludes. "She said she could hardly believe it." And she adds, as though it were irrelevant, "I think everyone is a little mad at Stella now for having died."

Ignoring that last (could she not have heard it? did Rachel not actually say it, only think it?), Day smiles; she is in love with this conversation. She now asks, "Did you notice Jimmy's sweater? Those stripes?"

"Exactly the color of Stella's hair. I saw that too."

"Do you think he thought of it?" Day is very serious.

"When he bought the sweater?" Rachel pauses before she answers. "No, I'm sure the choice was quite unconscious. But still."

"Yes, still. He did buy it." And Day smiles again, as though they had, together, understood and settled everything.

And Rachel, who feels that almost nothing has been understood, or settled, who herself does not see how she can get through the coming winter, much less the rest of her life—Rachel smiles back at her.

Barcelona

In the darkened, uneven cobbled square, in the old quarter of ·
Barcelona, the Barrio Gótico, the middle-aged American couple who walk by appear to be just that: American, middle-
aged. The man is tall and bald; his head shines dimly as he
and his wife cross the shaft of light from an open doorway.
She is smaller, with pale hair; she walks fast to keep up with
her husband. She is wearing gold chains, and they, too, shine
in the light. She carries a small bag in which there could be
—more gold? money? some interesting pills? They pass a
young Spaniard lounging in a corner whose face the man for
no reason takes note of.

Persis Fox, the woman, is a fairly successful illustrator,
beginning to be sought after by New York publishers, but
she sees herself as being in most ways a coward, a very fearful
person; she is afraid of planes, of high bridges, she is overly
worried by the illnesses of children—a rather boring list, as
she thinks of it. Some years ago she was afraid that Thad, her
husband, who teaches at Harvard, would take off with some
student, some dark, sexily athletic type from Texas, possibly.
More recently she has been frightened by accounts everywhere of muggings, robberies, rapes. She entirely believes in

the likelihood of nuclear war. She can and does lie awake at night with such thoughts, for frozen hours.

However, walking across these darkened cobbles, in the old quarter of Barcelona, toward a restaurant that Cambridge friends have recommended, she is not afraid at all, only interested in what she is seeing: just before the square, an arched and windowed walk up above the alley, now crenellated silhouettes, everywhere blackened old stones. Also, she is hungry, looking forward to the seafood for which this restaurant is famous. And she wishes that Thad would not walk so fast; by now he is about five feet ahead of her, in an alley.

In the next instant, though, before she has seen or heard any person approaching, someone is running past her in the dark—but not past; he is beside her, a tall dark boy, grabbing at her purse, pulling its short strap. Persis' first instinct is to let him have it, not because she is afraid—she is not, still not, afraid—but from a conditioned reflex, instructing her to give people what they want: children, her husband.

In the following second a more primitive response sets in, and she cries out, "No!"—as she thinks, Kindergarten, some little boy pulling a toy away. And next thinks, Not kindergarten. Spain. A thief.

He is stronger, and with a sudden sharp tug he wins; he has pulled the bag from her and run off, as Persis still yells, "No!"—and as (amazingly!) she remembers the word for thief. "LADRÓN!" she cries out. *"Ladrón!"*

Then suddenly Thad is back (Persis has not exactly thought of him in those seconds), and almost before she has finished saying "He took my bag!" Thad is running toward the square, where the thief went. Thad is running, running —so tall and fast, such a sprint, as though this were a marathon, or Memorial Drive, where he usually runs. He is off into the night, as Persis yells again, *"Ladrón!"* and she starts out after him.

Persis is wearing low boots (thank God), not heels, and she can hear Thad's whistle, something he does with two fingers in his mouth, intensely shrill, useful for summoning children from ski slopes or beaches as night comes on. Persis, also running, follows the sound. She comes at last to a fairly wide, dimly lit street where Thad is standing, breathing hard.

She touches his arm. "Thad—"

Still intent on the chase, he hardly looks at her. He is not doing this for her; it is something between men. He says, "I think he went that way."

"But Thad—"

The street down which he is pointing, and into which he now begins to stride, with Persis just following—this street's darkness is broken at intervals by the steamy yellow windows of shabby restaurants, the narrow open door of a bar. Here and there a few people stand in doorways, watching the progress of the Americans. Thad sticks his head into the restaurants, the bar. "I don't see him," he reports back each time.

Well, of course not. And of course each time Persis is glad —glad that the boy is hidden somewhere. Gone. Safe, as she and Thad are safe.

They reach the end of the block, when from behind them a voice calls out, in English, not loudly, "Lady, this your bag?"

Thad and Persis turn to see a dark, contemptuous young face, a tall boy standing in a doorway. Not, Thad later assures Persis, and later still their friends—not the thief, whom he saw as they first crossed the square, and would recognize. But a friend of his?

The boy kicks his foot at something on the cobbles, which Thad walks over to pick up, and which is Persis' bag.

"I can't believe it!" she cries out, aware of triteness, as Thad hands over the bag to her. But by now, now that everything is over, she is seriously frightened; inwardly she trembles.

"Well, we got it." Thad speaks calmly, but Persis can hear the pride in his voice, along with some nervousness. He is still breathing hard, but he has begun to walk with his purposeful stride again. "The restaurant must be down here," he tells her.

Astoundingly, it is; after a couple of turns they see the name on a red neon sign, the name of the place they have been told about, where they have made a reservation.

The kitchen seems to be in the front room, next to the bar: all steam and steel, noisy clanging. Smoke and people, glasses rattling, crashing. "I really need a drink," Persis tells Thad, as instead they are led back to a room full of tables, people —many Americans, tourists, all loud and chattering.

At their small table, waiting for wine, with his tight New England smile Thad asks, "Aren't you going to check it? See what's still there?"

Curiously, this has not yet occurred to Persis as something to be done; she has simply clutched the bag. Now, as she looks down at the bag on her lap, it seems shabbier, a battered survivor. Obediently she unsnaps the flap. "Oh good, my passport's here," she tells Thad.

"That's great." He is genuinely pleased with himself— and why should he not be, having behaved with such courage? Then he frowns. "He got all your money?"

"Well no, actually there wasn't any money. I keep it in my pocket. Always, when I go to New York, that's what I do."

Why does Thad look so confused just then? A confusion of emotions is spread across his fair, lined face. He is disappointed, somehow? Upset that he ran after a thief who had stolen a bag containing so little? Upset that Persis, who now goes down to New York on publishing business by herself, has tricks for self-preservation?

Sipping wine, and almost instantly dizzy, light in her head, Persis tries to explain herself. "Men are such dopes," she heedlessly starts. "They always think that women carry everything they own in their bags. Thieves think that, I mean. So I just shove money and credit cards into some pocket. There's only makeup in my bags."

"And your passport." Stern, judicious Thad.

"Oh yes, of course," Persis babbles. "That would have been terrible. We could have spent days in offices."

Gratified, sipping at his wine, Thad says, "I wonder why he didn't take it, actually."

Persis does not say, "Because it's hidden inside my address book"—although quite possibly that was the case. Instead, she says what is also surely true: "Because you scared him. The last thing he expected was someone running after him, and that *whistle*."

Thad smiles, and his face settles into a familiar expression: that of a generally secure, intelligent man, a lucky person, for whom things happen more or less as he would expect them to.

Persis is thinking, and not for the first time, how terrible it must be to be a man, how terrifying. Men are always running, chasing something. And if you are rich and successful, like Thad, you have to hunt down anyone who wants to take away your possessions. Or if you're poor, down on your luck, you might be tempted to chase after a shabby bag that holds nothing of any real value, to snatch such a bag from a foreign woman who is wearing false gold chains that shine and glimmer in the dark.

Separate Planes

In the Mexico City airport, in the upstairs bar adjacent to the
waiting room for planes to various Mexican cities—Oaxaca,
Ixtapa, Mérida—three highly conspicuous Americans are
having a drink together, attracting considerable attention
from other, mostly Mexican travellers. They are a young man
and a somewhat older married couple; in some indefinable
way the couple look long married, which they are. The young
man, who is actually in early middle age, still appreciably
younger than the other two—this man is the most conven-
tionally dressed of the three: khaki pants, navy blazer, white
shirt. Sheer physical beauty is what draws so many looks to
him, especially in Mexico, among dark people: his sleek flat
blond hair shines, even in this ill-lit room; his narrow eyes
are intensely blue, his teeth of a dazzling whiteness. He is a
tennis instructor at a small college in Southern California,
and he is going from Oaxaca, where all three of these people
just have been, on to Ixtapa, where there is to be a tournament at the Club Med. His name is Hugh Cornelisen.

Of the older two, who are headed for Mérida, the man is
the more flamboyant, as to costume. Tall, excessively thin,
with thinning, grayish hair and a reddish face, he is wearing

a pink linen suit, an ascot of darker pink silk. His gestures
are slightly overanimated. Behind heavy horn-rimmed glasses
his dark eyes blink a lot. His face is deeply furrowed; deep
lines run down his cheeks and across his forehead—perhaps from a lifetime of serious thought, deep contemplation,
and possibly more than his share of conflicts, sharp torments
of the heart. He is Allen Rodgers, a lawyer, from New
Haven.

His wife, Alexandra, is a woman of considerable size—a
wonderful size, actually; her height and her general massive-
ness convey strength and power. She is unaware, though, of
the impression she makes—she wishes she were smaller. She
has great dark, golden eyes, and black, gray-streaked hair
pulled into a knot. A long time ago, in the forties, she was
studying Greek literature at Yale; she and Allen met at
various New Haven parties—an older (ten years) man, a
tall, uneasy girl. And actually she looks better now than she
did as a very young woman; then she was awkward with her
size, shy, and overeager in her mania for knowledge, her greed
for love. Now, especially in her brown, loosely woven dress,
with her big purple beads, big gold earrings, Alexandra looks
majestic—but at this moment she is thinking that she would
give everything she has if she could be young again, even for
just a couple of days; then, just possibly, she would be going
off to Ixtapa with Hugh, instead of to Mérida with Allen. At
this moment she does not see how she can bear the rest of
her life with Hugh's face absent from it.

On second thought, though, she does not really wish that
she could go to Ixtapa with Hugh—complications, embar-
rassments. She would only like him to kiss her, preferably in
the dark, where she is invisible.

Alexandra's quest for love did not end after her marriage to
Allen, although she had hoped (they both hoped) that she

would change. At first there were just a few excited flurries, kitchen kisses, some passionate gropings in cars, after summer parties in Vermont, where they and many of their friends had lakeside cottages. Then there was a serious, real affair with a younger colleague of Allen's, cautiously, rather guardedly begun as a summer romance but continued with frenzied meetings in New York hotels, in motels along the turnpike. This left everyone involved raw and shaken (Alexandra had been forced or felt herself forced to tell Allen almost all about it.). After that she "drifted into," as she put it to herself, a couple of not very serious dalliances; she found the very contrast between these connections and the high seriousness of her first affair depressing, and she resolved not to do that again. But then she did. All of which was at least suspected by Allen, if unclearly.

Her Greek studies have more or less lapsed, although she still tries an occasional translation; some of her translated poems have been published in literary journals.

In what Allen describes as his own "declining years" he has experienced a series of critically painful "crushes" on young women, usually students, always beautiful. Analysis of these feelings has been a source of further pain, a scalpel applied to a wound, but he has achieved a certain understanding of his feelings: he has come to understand that all he wants of these young women is sometimes to *see* them, but "want" is an imprecise word for his wild craving, his need.

The most recent object of this "surely most unwanted affection," as Allen might say, were he able to talk about it— the most recent "crush" has been on a tall, pale red-haired girl, Mona, from Colorado. Mona, with milk-white, unfreckled skin, wide light-blue eyes, and endless legs, which she carelessly, restlessly crossed and recrossed, all summer long, in her white tennis shorts. Mona was in New Haven visiting the daughter of friends, making everything worse, more "social." A feminist, she planned to go to law school, and she liked to talk to Allen about law. "I think she has a sort of crush on you," Alexandra imperceptively remarked, at the start of summer. "Well, feminists get crushes too," he limply countered.

Later, seeming to catch some hint of his actual feelings, Alexandra stopped mentioning Mona altogether.

Alexandra and Allen met Hugh because they were all staying in the same hotel in Oaxaca—a beautiful converted convent, with open courtyards full of flowers, lovely long cloisters, and everywhere birds. Arriving there on an early-morning plane from Mexico City, registering at the desk, as they were led toward their room, Alexandra and Allen exchanged smiles of pure pleasure at the beauty of it all, the sweet freshness of the air, such a contrast to Mexico City or New Haven. They liked their room, which was white-plastered, very clean, with a low slant ceiling, a window looking out to an ancient well, of soft gray stone. As they stood there just within the doorway, taking everything in, a young blond American in khaki walking shorts passed by; he looked in, smiled quickly in their direction.

After a little unpacking Alexandra and Allen walked up to the neighboring church, whose annex was a museum of costumes and artifacts, and there was the blond young man again, before a display of ferocious armaments, feathered headdresses. Seeing them, he gave another smile; they all smiled, acknowledging the coincidence.

At lunch, in the sunny, vine-hung courtyard, a haven for butterflies and hummingbirds, there he was again, but at a table some distance from theirs. More smiles.

And late in the afternoon, after more walking about, a little shopping, sightseeing, the blond young man was just across the pool, sunning himself, as he glanced through a magazine. He waved in their direction; they returned the gesture.

"Odd that he's alone," Alexandra murmured. "He's really quite *beau*."

"Oh, he's probably saving himself for something. He looks athletic."

"I wonder what."

Allen speculated. "Well, something graceful. Something not, as the kids say, gross. Golf? Maybe tennis?"

That night, after a fairly long siesta—though they were both troubled sleepers, often restless—Alexandra and Allen came into the bar rather late to find almost all the tables occupied, and there *he* was, standing up at the sight of them, saying, "Well, we seem to be on the same schedule, don't we? Won't you folks join me for a drink?"

Close up, even in that darkish bar, Hugh turned out to be somewhat less young than they at first had thought; still, he was considerably younger than they were, and his general air was boyish—to Alexandra, privately, he remained "the young blond." As they exchanged names and certain identifying facts—home bases, previous trips to Mexico, next destinations—professions were brought out last, and Hugh seemed impressed by theirs: a lawyer and a scholar, of Greek! He was very pleased at Allen's guess as to tennis for himself.

"Allen's terrifically intuitive," explained Alexandra.

"Oh, I believe you!" A flash of teeth.

"Mostly I'm very observant." Dry Allen.

They passed a pleasant, noncommittal evening together, going off early to their separate rooms.

And, the next morning, there was Hugh, arriving for breakfast at the exact moment of their arrival.

Unlike either Allen or Alexandra, Hugh was an intensely physical person, a man much at home in his body, exuding animal energy. He even looked at things in a total, physical way, as animals do, all his muscles at attention, along with his depthless, clear blue eyes. On their one planned excursion together, in a rented car, out to the ruins at Monte Albán, the ancient pyramids, instead of looking at the stones Alexandra mostly watched Hugh, as he paced and bent and stopped to look, turned and bent down again. (And Allen watched Alexandra, watching.)

And their odd synchroneity continued. Even when Allen and Alexandra slept somewhat late and were late coming in to breakfast, there would be Hugh, saying ruefully that he had overslept. They laughed about it, this coincidence of inner timing, but even as they did so Alexandra felt a tiny chill of fear: suppose they should come into a room, as they surely would, sooner or later, and not find Hugh? Coming into the bar and finding him there at night, smiling and standing up at the sight of them, saying, "This is my first Margarita, honest"—coming on Hugh in that way became for Alexandra like finding a sudden brilliant light, in anticipated darkness.

Now they are drinking what are probably their last Margaritas, in this huge, dingy, crowded area, among their own and other people's piles of luggage, these somewhat unlikely, not quite friends (although not unlikely to the mostly shabby Mexicans who are with them in the waiting room, who stare and find it perfectly reasonable that these three Hollywood-looking Americans should be together).

In a summing-up way Hugh says, "Well, it certainly was lucky for me, running into you folks down there."

"Oh, lucky for us!" Allen responds very quickly, with a lively smile.

"Oh, lucky!" Alexandra echoes, her own smile a little uncertain.

Hugh's face is bright as, having covered that topic, he

moves on to more urgent matters. "I guess planes are always late getting out of here?" he questions. "No counting on schedules?"

Allen answers, "Probably not. Schedules are, uh, almost irrelevant."

Hugh's plane for Ixtapa was originally scheduled to leave an hour after that of Allen and Alexandra for Mérida; however, both schedules have continuously changed, so that now the question of who leaves when is quite "up in the air," as Allen has put it, to a dutiful smile from Alexandra, a brief but appreciative chuckle from Hugh.

Now, though, as they regard the shifting numbers on the elevated blackboard, it appears that Hugh will leave first. Alexandra has all along known that this would be the case.

And, finally, his plane is announced. Boarding time.

In a suddenly awkward cluster the three of them stand up, not quite facing each other.

Allen, as he always uncontrollably does when ill at ease, begins to talk. "Well, I hope your tournament—this short flight—not too late," he says, almost unheard in the general mounting confusion of people moving toward a just forming, straggling line, Spanish voices raised in prolonged farewells, bodies momentarily clutched in parting embraces.

Hugh grasps Allen's hand, and presses it for an instant. What he indistinctly says is *"Swell."*

Turning to Alexandra, so large and helpless, Hugh seems to see or simply to feel some nuance that moves him, somehow. Quickly bending toward her, he kisses her lightly on each cheek (a most un-Hugh-like gesture, Allen thinks) as he says, "Like the French! Well, Alexandra, so long!" and he turns and walks quickly, jauntily, into the crowd, toward the now moving line, in the huge and dingy, barely illuminated room.

Leaving them there.

Molly's Dog

Accustomed to extremes of mood, which she experienced less as "swings" than as plunges, or more rarely as soarings, Molly Harper, a newly retired screenwriter, was nevertheless quite overwhelmed by the blackness—the horror, really, with which, one dark pre-dawn hour, she viewed a minor trip, a jaunt from San Francisco to Carmel, to which she had very much looked forward. It was to be a weekend, simply, at an inn where in fact she had often stayed before, with various lovers (Molly's emotional past had been strenuous). This time she was to travel with Sandy Norris, an old non-lover friend, who owned a bookstore. (Sandy usually had at least a part-time lover of his own, one in a series of nice young men.)

Before her film job, and her move to Los Angeles, Molly had been a poet, a good one—even, one year, a Yale Younger Poet. But she was living, then, from hand to mouth, from one idiot job to another. (Sandy was a friend from that era; they began as neighbors in a shabby North Beach apartment building, now long-since demolished.) As she had approached middle age, though, being broke all the time seemed undignified, if not downright scary. It wore her down, and she

grabbed at the film work and moved down to L.A. Some
years of that life were wearing in another way, she found, and
she moved from Malibu back up to San Francisco, with a little saved money, and her three beautiful, cross old cats. And
hopes for a new and calmer life. She meant to start seriously
writing again.

In her pre-trip waking nightmare, though, which was convincing in the way that such an hour's imaginings always are
(one sees the truth, and sees that any sunnier ideas are chi-
merical, delusions) at three, or four a.m., Molly pictured the
two of them, as they would be in tawdry, ridiculous Carmel:
herself, a scrawny sun-dried older woman, and Sandy, her
wheezing, chain-smoking fat queer friend. There would be
some silly awkwardness about sleeping arrangements, and
instead of making love they would drink too much.

And, fatally, she thought of another weekend, in that
same inn, years back: she remembered entering one of the
cabins with a lover, and as soon as he, the lover, had closed
the door they had turned to each other and kissed, had
laughed and hurried off to bed. Contrast enough to make her
nearly weep—and she knew, too, at four in the morning,
that her cherished view of a meadow, and the river, the sea,
would now be blocked by condominiums, or something.

This trip, she realized too late, at dawn, was to represent
a serious error in judgment, one more in a lifetime of dark
mistakes. It would weigh down and quite possibly sink her
friendship with Sandy, and she put a high value on friendship. Their one previous lapse, hers and Sandy's, which occurred when she stopped smoking and he did not (according
to Sandy she had been most unpleasant about it, and perhaps she had been), had made Molly extremely unhappy.

But, good friends as she and Sandy were, why on earth a
weekend together? The very frivolousness with which this
plan had been hit upon seemed ominous; simply, Sandy had

said that funnily enough he had never been to Carmel, and Molly had said that she knew a nifty place to stay. And so, why not? they said. A long time ago, when they both were poor, either of them would have given anything for such a weekend (though not with each other) and perhaps that was how things should be, Molly judged, at almost five. And she thought of all the poor lovers, who could never go anywhere at all, who quarrel from sheer claustrophobia.

Not surprisingly, the next morning Molly felt considerably better, although imperfectly rested. But with almost her accustomed daytime energy she set about getting ready for the trip, doing several things simultaneously, as was her tendency: packing clothes and breakfast food (the cabins were equipped with little kitchens, she remembered), straightening up her flat and arranging the cats' quarters on her porch.

By two in the afternoon, the hour established for their departure, Molly was ready to go, if a little sleepy; fatigue had begun to cut into her energy. Well, she was not twenty any more, or thirty or forty, even, she told herself, tolerantly.

Sandy telephoned at two-fifteen. In his raspy voice he apologized; his assistant had been late getting in, he still had a couple of things to do. He would pick her up at three, three-thirty at the latest.

Irritating: Molly had sometimes thought that Sandy's habitual lateness was his way of establishing control; at other times she thought that he was simply tardy, as she herself was punctual (but why?). However, wanting a good start to their weekend, she told him that that was really okay; it did not matter what time they got to Carmel, did it?

She had begun a rereading of *Howards End,* which she planned to take along, and now she found that the book was even better than she remembered it as being, from the wonderful assurance of the first sentence, "One may as well begin with Helen's letters to her sister—" Sitting in her sunny window, with her sleeping cats, Molly managed to be wholly absorbed in her reading—not in waiting for Sandy, nor in thinking, especially, of Carmel.

Just past four he arrived at her door: Sandy, in his pressed blue blazer, thin hair combed flat, his reddish face bright. Letting him in, brushing cheeks in the kiss of friends, Molly thought how nice he looked, after all: his kind blue eyes, sad witty mouth.

He apologized for lateness. "I absolutely had to take a shower," he said, with his just-crooked smile.

"Well, it's really all right. I'd begun *Howards End* again. I'd forgotten how wonderful it is."

"Oh well. *Forster.*"

Thus began one of the rambling conversations, more bookish gossip than "literary," which formed, perhaps, the core of their friendship, its reliable staple. In a scattered way they ran about, conversationally, among favorite old novels, discussing characters not quite as intimates but certainly as contemporaries, as alive. *Was* Margaret Schlegel somewhat prudish? Sandy felt that she was; Molly took a more sympathetic view of her shyness. Such talk, highly pleasurable and reassuring to them both, carried Molly and Sandy, in his small green car, past the dull first half of their trip: down the Bayshore Highway, past San Jose and Gilroy, and took them to where (Molly well remembered) it all became beautiful. Broad stretches of bright green early summer fields; distant hills, grayish-blue; and then islands of sweeping dark live oaks.

At the outskirts of Carmel itself a little of her pre-dawn apprehension came back to Molly, as they drove past those imitation Cotswold cottages, fake-Spanish haciendas, or bright little gingerbread houses. And the main drag, Ocean

Avenue, with its shops, shops—all that tweed and pewter, "imported" jams and tea. More tourists than ever before, of course, in their bright synthetic tourist clothes, their bulging shopping bags—Japanese, French, German, English tourists, taking home their awful wares.

"You turn left next, on Dolores," Molly instructed, and then heard herself begin nervously to babble. "Of course if the place has really been wrecked we don't have to stay for two nights, do we. We could go on down to Big Sur, or just go home, for heaven's sake."

"In any case, sweetie, if they've wrecked it, it won't be your fault." Sandy laughed, and wheezed, and coughed. He had been smoking all the way down, which Molly had succeeded in not mentioning.

Before them, then, was their destination: the inn, with its clump of white cottages. And the meadow. So far, nothing that Molly could see had changed. No condominiums. Everything as remembered.

They were given the cabin farthest from the central office, the one nearest the meadow, and the river and the sea. A small bedroom, smaller kitchen, and in the living room a studio couch. Big windows, and that view.

"Obviously, the bedroom is yours," Sandy magnanimously declared, plunking down his bag on the studio couch.

"*Well*," was all for the moment that Molly could say, as she put her small bag down in the bedroom, and went into the kitchen with the sack of breakfast things. From the little window she looked out to the meadow, saw that it was pink now with wildflowers, in the early June dusk. Three large brown cows were grazing out there, near where the river must be. Farther out she could see the wide, gray-white strip of beach, and the dark blue, turbulent sea. On the other side of the meadow were soft green hills, on which—yes, one might have known—new houses had arisen. But somehow inoffensively; they blended. And beyond the beach was the sharp, rocky silhouette of Point Lobos, crashing waves, leaping foam. All blindingly undiminished: a miraculous gift.

Sandy came into the kitchen, bearing bottles. Beaming Sandy, saying, "Mol, this is the most divine place. We must celebrate your choice. Immediately."

They settled in the living room with their drinks, with that view before them: the almost imperceptibly graying sky, the meadow, band of sand, the sea.

And, as she found that she often did, with Sandy, Molly began to say what had just come into her mind. "You wouldn't believe how stupid I was, as a very young woman," she prefaced, laughing a little. "Once I came down here with a lawyer, from San Francisco, terribly rich. Quite famous, actually." (The same man with whom she had so quickly rushed off to bed, on their arrival—as she did not tell Sandy.) "Married, of course. The first part of my foolishness. And I was really broke at the time—*broke,* I was poor as hell, being a typist to support my poetry habit. You remember. But I absolutely insisted on bringing all the food for that stolen, illicit weekend, can you imagine? What on earth was I trying to prove? Casseroles of crabmeat, endive for salads. Honestly, how crazy I was!"

Sandy laughed agreeably, and remarked a little plaintively that for him she had only brought breakfast food. But he was not especially interested in that old, nutty view of her, Molly saw—and resolved that that would be her last "past" story. Customarily they did not discuss their love affairs.

She asked, "Shall we walk out on the beach tomorrow?"

"But of course."

Later they drove to a good French restaurant, where they drank a little too much wine, but they did not get drunk. And their two reflections, seen in a big mirror across the tiny room, looked perfectly all right: Molly, gray-haired, dark-eyed and thin, in her nice flowered silk dress; and Sandy, tidy and alert, a small plump man, in a neat navy blazer.

After dinner they drove along the beach, the cold white sand ghostly in the moonlight. Past enormous millionaire houses, and blackened windbent cypresses. Past the broad sloping river beach, and then back to their cabin, with its huge view of stars.

In her narrow bed, in the very small but private bedroom, Molly thought again, for a little while, of that very silly early self of hers: how eagerly self-defeating she had been—how foolish, in love. But she felt a certain tolerance now for that young person, herself, and she even smiled as she thought of all that intensity, that driven waste of emotion. In many ways middle age is preferable, she thought.

In the morning, they met the dog.

After breakfast they had decided to walk on the river beach, partly since Molly remembered that beach as being far less populated than the main beach was. Local families brought their children there. Or their dogs, or both.

Despite its visibility from their cabin, the river beach was actually a fair distance off, and so instead of walking there they drove, for maybe three or four miles. They parked and got out, and were pleased to see that no one else was there. Just a couple of dogs, who seemed not to be there together: a plumy, oversized friendly Irish setter, who ran right over to Molly and Sandy; and a smaller, long-legged, thin-tailed dark gray dog, with very tall ears—a shy young dog, who kept her distance, running a wide circle around them, after the setter had ambled off somewhere else. As they neared the water, the gray dog sidled over to sniff at them, her ears flattened, seeming to indicate a lowering of suspicion. She allowed herself to be patted, briefly; she seemed to smile.

Molly and Sandy walked near the edge of the water; the dog ran ahead of them.

The day was glorious, windy, bright blue, and perfectly clear; they could see the small pines and cypresses that struggled to grow from the steep sharp rocks of Point Lobos, could see fishing boats far out on the deep azure ocean. From time to time the dog would run back in their direction, and then she would rush toward a receding wave, chasing it backward in a seeming happy frenzy. Assuming her (then) to live nearby, Molly almost enviously wondered at her sheer delight in what must be familiar. The dog barked at each wave, and ran after every one as though it were something new and marvellous.

Sandy picked up a stick and threw it forward. The dog ran after the stick, picked it up and shook it several times, and then, in a tentative way, she carried it back toward Sandy and Molly—not dropping it, though. Sandy had to take it from her mouth. He threw it again, and the dog ran off in that direction.

The wind from the sea was strong, and fairly chilling. Molly wished she had a warmer sweater, and she chided herself: she could have remembered that Carmel was cold, along with her less practical memories. She noted that Sandy's ears were red, and saw him rub his hands together. But she thought, I hope he won't want to leave soon, it's so beautiful. And such a nice dog. (Just that, at that moment: a very nice dog.)

The dog, seeming for the moment to have abandoned the stick game, rushed at a just-alighted flock of sea gulls, who then rose from the wet waves' edge and with what must have been (to a dog) a most gratifying flapping of wings, with cluckings of alarm.

Molly and Sandy were now close to the mouth of the river,

the gorge cut into the beach, as water emptied into the sea. Impossible to cross—although Molly could remember when one could, when she and whatever companion had jumped easily over some water, and had then walked much farther down the beach. Now she and Sandy simply stopped there, and regarded the newish houses that were built up on the nearby hills. And they said to each other:

"What a view those people must have!"

"Actually the houses aren't too bad."

"There must be some sort of design control."

"I'm sure."

"Shall we buy a couple? A few million should take care of it."

"Oh sure, let's."

They laughed.

They turned around to find the dog waiting for them, in a dog's classic pose of readiness: her forelegs outstretched in the sand, rump and tail up in the air. Her eyes brown and intelligent, appraising, perhaps affectionate.

"Sandy, throw her another stick."

"You do it this time."

"Well, I don't throw awfully well."

"Honestly, Mol, she won't mind."

Molly poked through a brown tangle of seaweed and small broken sticks, somewhat back from the waves. The only stick that would do was too long, but she picked it up and threw it anyway. It was true that she did not throw very well, and the wind made a poor throw worse: the stick landed only a few feet away. But the dog ran after it, and then ran about with the stick in her mouth, shaking it, holding it high up as she ran, like a trophy.

Sandy and Molly walked more slowly now, against the wind. To their right was the meadow, across which they could just make out the cottages where they were staying. Ahead was a cluster of large, many-windowed ocean-front houses—in one of which, presumably, their dog lived.

Once their walk was over, they had planned to go into Carmel and buy some wine and picnic things, and to drive out into the valley for lunch. They began to talk about this now, and then Sandy said that first he would like to go by the Mission. "I've never seen it," he explained.

"Oh well, sure."

From time to time on that return walk one or the other of them would pick up a stick and throw it for the dog, who sometimes lost a stick and then looked back to them for another, who stayed fairly near them but maintained, still, a certain shy independence.

She was wearing a collar (Molly and Sandy were later to reassure each other as to this) but at that time, on the beach, neither of them saw any reason to examine it. Besides, the dog never came quite that close. It would have somehow seemed presumptuous to grab her and read her collar's inscription.

In a grateful way Molly was thinking, again, how reliable the beauty of that place had turned out to be: their meadow view, and now the river beach.

They neared the parking lot, and Sandy's small green car.

An older woman, heavy and rather bent, was just coming into the lot, walking her toy poodle, on a leash. *Their* dog ran over for a restrained sniff, and then ambled back to where Molly and Sandy were getting into the car.

"Pretty dog!" the woman called out to them. "I never saw one with such long ears!"

"Yes—she's not ours."

"She isn't lost, is she?"

"Oh no, she has a collar."

Sandy started up the car; he backed up and out of the

parking lot, slowly. Glancing back, Molly saw that the dog seemed to be leaving too, heading home, probably.

But a few blocks later—by then Sandy was driving somewhat faster—for some reason Molly looked back again, and there was the dog. Still. Racing. Following them.

She looked over to Sandy and saw that he too had seen the dog, in the rear view mirror.

Feeling her glance, apparently, he frowned. "She'll go home in a minute," he said.

Molly closed her eyes, aware of violent feelings within herself, somewhere: anguish? dread? She could no more name them than she could locate the emotion.

She looked back again, and there was the dog, although she was now much farther—hopelessly far behind them. A small gray dot. Racing. Still.

Sandy turned right in the direction of the Mission, as they had planned. They drove past placid houses with their beds of too-bright, unnatural flowers, too yellow or too pink. Clean glass windows, neat shingles. Trim lawns. Many houses, all much alike, and roads, and turns in roads.

As they reached the Mission, its parking area was crowded with tour busses, campers, vans, and ordinary cars.

There was no dog behind them.

"You go on in," Molly said. "I've seen it pretty often. I'll wait out here in the sun."

She seated herself on a stone bench near the edge of the parking area—in the sun, beside a bright clump of bougainvillea, and she told herself that by now, surely, the dog had turned around and gone on home, or back to the beach. And that even if she and Sandy had turned and gone back to her, or stopped and waited for her, eventually they would have had to leave her, somewhere.

Sandy came out, unenthusiastic about the church, and they drove into town to buy sandwiches and wine.

In the grocery store, where everything took a very long time, it occurred to Molly that probably they should have checked back along the river beach road, just to make sure that the dog was no longer there. But by then it was too late.

They drove out into the valley; they found a nice sunny place for a picnic, next to the river, the river that ran on to their beach, and the sea. After a glass of wine Molly was able to ask, "You don't really think she was lost, do you?"

But why would Sandy know, any more than she herself did? At that moment Molly hated her habit of dependence on men for knowledge—any knowledge, any man. But at least, for the moment, he was kind. "Oh, I really don't think so," he said. "She's probably home by now." And he mentioned the collar.

Late that afternoon, in the deepening, cooling June dusk, the river beach was diminishingly visible from their cabin, where Molly and Sandy sat with their pre-dinner drinks. At first, from time to time, it was possible to see people walking out there: small stick figures, against a mild pink sunset sky. Once, Molly was sure that one of the walkers had a dog along. But it was impossible, at that distance, and in the receding light, to identify an animal's markings, or the shape of its ears.

They had dinner in the inn's long dining room, from which it was by then too dark to see the beach. They drank too much, and they had a silly outworn argument about Sandy's smoking, during which he accused her of being bossy; she said that he was inconsiderate.

Waking at some time in the night, from a shallow, winey sleep, Molly thought of the dog out there on the beach, how cold it must be, by now—the hard chilled sand and stinging waves. From her bed she could hear the sea's relentless crash.

The pain that she experienced then was as familiar as it was acute.

They had said that they would leave fairly early on Sunday morning and go home by way of Santa Cruz: a look at the town, maybe lunch, and a brief tour of the university there. And so, after breakfast, Molly and Sandy began to pull their belongings together.

Tentatively (but was there a shade of mischief, of teasing in his voice? Could he sense what she was feeling?) Sandy asked, "I guess we won't go by the river beach?"

"No."

They drove out from the inn, up and onto the highway; they left Carmel. But as soon as they were passing Monterey, Pacific Grove, it began to seem intolerable to Molly that they had not gone back to the beach. Although she realized that either seeing or *not* seeing the dog would have been terrible.

If she now demanded that Sandy turn around and go back, would he do it? Probably not, she concluded; his face had a set, stubborn look. But Molly wondered about that, off and on, all the way to Santa Cruz.

For lunch they had sandwiches in a rather scruffy, open-air place; they drove up to and in and around the handsome, almost deserted university; and then, anxious not to return to the freeway, they took off on a road whose sign listed, among other destinations, San Francisco.

Wild Country: thickly wooded, steeply mountainous. Occasionally through an opening in the trees they could glimpse some sheer cliff, gray sharp rocks; once a distant small green secret meadow. A proper habitat for mountain lions, Molly thought, or deer, at least, and huge black birds. "It reminds me of something," she told Sandy, disconsolately. "Maybe even some place I've only read about."

"Or a movie," he agreed. "God knows it's melodramatic."

Then Molly remembered: it was indeed a movie that this savage scenery made her think of, and a movie that she herself had done the screenplay for. About a quarrelling, alcoholic couple, Americans, who were lost in wild Mexican mountains. As she had originally written it, they remained lost, presumably to die there. Only, the producer saw fit to change all that, and he had them romantically rescued by some good-natured Mexican bandits.

They had reached a crossroads, where there were no signs at all. The narrow, white roads all led off into the woods. To Molly, the one on the right looked most logical, as a choice, and she said so, but Sandy took the middle one. "You really like to be in charge, don't you," he rather unpleasantly remarked, lighting a cigarette.

There had been a lot of news in the local papers about a murderer who attacked and then horribly killed hikers and campers, in those very Santa Cruz mountains, Molly suddenly thought. She rolled up her window and locked the door, and she thought again of the ending of her movie. She tended to believe that one's fate, or doom, had a certain logic to it; even, that it was probably written out somewhere, even if by one's self. Most lives, including their endings, made a certain sort of sense, she thought.

The gray dog then came back powerfully, vividly to her mind: the small heart pounding in that thin, narrow ribcage, as she ran after their car. Unbearable: Molly's own heart hurt, as she closed her eyes and tightened her hands into fists.

"Well, Christ," exploded Sandy, at that moment. "We've come to a dead end. Look!"

They had; the road ended abruptly, it simply stopped, in a heavy grove of cypresses and redwoods. There was barely space to turn around.

Not saying, "Why didn't you take the other road?" Molly

imagined them to be a family, two brothers with
[..]ter, and she thought she had never seen such glamor-
[..]h quintessentially *California* people. Small dark
[..]from Quincy, Mass., on a scholarship, was dazzled,
[..]emained dazzled after they met—or, rather, after
[..]ric (at a swimming party at Lake Lagunitas, of all
[..]nstances; Eric said she looked like a goldfish, in
[..]ellow bathing suit). She and Eric fell in love, and
[..]ed her to his twin sister, Joan, in medical school
[..]him and married. And she met Joan's husband,
[..]ing physics.

[..]addition to their similar looks, those three have
[..]mon. Miriam, who studied English, now does
[..] at the public library in Seattle, where she
[..]moved. However, it is Miriam who has, just
[..]urch, a weird science-fiction thought: she
[..]e dust particles in Mexico could be silicon
[..]ed for some violence. She thinks that any-
[..]happen there, and she is suddenly afraid.
[..]ehind the others, Miriam then notices a
[..]deeply recessed niche. Even in those dark
[..]e can see that the sagging figure of the
[..]lcod; red blood (well, paint, of course)
[..] gaping wound, just below his ribs.
[..]eripheral vision catch that image, that
[..]strange, quite uncharacteristic thought
[..]e? She is not sure, not then or later
[..]verything.

[..] really—Miriam finds it wonderful
[..]se others, to be with them. When
[..] even, a sense of being assimilated
[..]hem. It is as if by sufficiently gaz-

instead cried out, uncontrollably, "But why didn't we go back
for the dog?"

"Jesus, Molly." Redfaced with the effort he was making,
Sandy glared. "That's what we most need right now. Some
stray bitch in the car with us."

"What do you mean, stray bitch? She chose us—she
wanted to come with us."

"How stupid you are! I had no idea."

"You're so selfish!" she shouted.

Totally silent, then, in the finally righted but possibly
still lost car, they stared at each other: a moment of pure
dislike.

And then, "Three mangy cats, and now you want a dog,"
Sandy muttered. He started off, too fast, in the direction of
the crossroads. At which they made another turn.

Silently they travelled through more woods, past more
steep gorges and ravines, on the road that Molly had thought
they should have taken in the first place.

She had been right; they soon came to a group of signs
which said that they were heading toward Saratoga. They
were neither to die in the woods nor to be rescued by bandits.
Nor murdered. And, some miles past Saratoga, Molly apologized. "Actually I have a sort of a headache," she lied.

"I'm sorry, too, Mol. And you know I like your cats."
Which was quite possibly also a lie.

They got home safely, of course.

But somehow, after that trip, their friendship, Molly and
Sandy's, either "lapsed" again, or perhaps it was permanently
diminished; Molly was not sure. One or the other of them
would forget to call, until days or weeks had gone by, and
then their conversation would be guilty, apologetic.

And at first, back in town, despite the familiar and comforting presences of her cats, Molly continued to think with a painful obsessiveness of that beach dog, especially in early hours of sleeplessness. She imagined going back to Carmel alone to look for her; of advertising in the Carmel paper, describing a young female with gray markings. Tall ears.

However, she did none of those things. She simply went on with her calm new life, as before, with her cats. She wrote some poems.

But, although she had ceased to be plagued by her vision of the dog (running, endlessly running, growing smaller in the distance) she did not forget her.

And she thought of Carmel, now, in a vaguely painful way, as a place where she had lost, or left something of infinite value. A place to which she would not go back.

Mexican

Four North
interior of a
shabby but
and intric
flowers, a
tiptoe: t
follow
Miria
ston

h

Miria
their si
ous, su
Miriam,
and she
she met
odd circu
her small y
he introduc
along with
Russell, stud
And so, in
science in con
volunteer wor
and Eric have
then, in the ch
thinks that all t
chips, programm
thing at all could
Still tiptoeing
small crucifix, in a
shadows, though, s
Christ is lined with
seeps down from the
Or did Miriam's p
blood, just before her
about dust and violen
on, when she considers

Usually—almost always
to be associated with th
she is with them she has
by them, with them, into

ing up at them, at Eric, Joan, and Russell, she could absorb —could take on their qualities, even their blondness and height.

And in their separate and collective ways they cherish her, too, Miriam feels; even her differences from themselves are appreciated. "How small you are!" Eric sometimes laughingly, lovingly remarks, even now, after eight years of marriage. And Joan: "What heaven it must be to shop for size-3 clothes!"

It has sometimes occurred to Miriam, though, that she could do with fewer remarks about her size; so much attention to it makes her feel rather like their mascot. She is simply small, a fact not terribly interesting to herself.

And she does have to argue with them all, when the four are together, about her library volunteer work, her arguments being the obvious ones: tax cuts are killing the libraries, libraries need all the help they can get. And, she adds, with only a B.A. in English lit., what sort of job could she get these days? Also, Eric's cardiology practice brings in plenty of money. Everything she says is true, they have to agree. Still, they all—especially Joan (who earns more than either Eric or Russell)—seem to wish that she did something else. That she had a career.

Being alone with Eric is not at all the same as being with Eric and Joan and Russell; of course not. Alone, in Seattle, Miriam and Eric have domestic conversations: what needs to be fixed (their house is old, and large). And food: big Eric eats a lot, and on her way home from the library Miriam often stops to shop at the Pike Place Market (she loves it there, the beautiful open displays); Eric likes to hear about that, what she saw, what looked best. Their dinners are the high points of their days.

She occasionally feels, though, that Eric is more himself
when they are with Joan and Russell than when there are
only the two of them. With Joan and Russell, Eric talks
more, expresses opinions, makes jokes. Mostly medical jokes.
(Russell collects dirty limericks; he knows thousands.)

However, since Eric and Miriam have been in Seattle, they
see Joan and Russell considerably less, Joan's practice being
in Palo Alto; Russell works on the linear accelerator, at
Stanford.

But they still have these trips: by tradition the four of
them take vacations together. Joan and Russell do not come
up to Seattle; they have let it be known that they really can't
stand the Northwest. Miriam has not let it be known that
she is not truly fond of San Francisco, where they sometimes
meet. Everything so pretty, so "cute," she thinks, and does
not say. She also thinks (silently) that cable cars are dangerous. But: one year a barge trip in France, another the small
towns of Umbria and Tuscany. Last year Scotland, this year
Mexico.

Miriam's features are rather small, and her face has a curious
flatness to it. A small mask. Dark eyes in shallow sockets,
freckles across unprominent cheekbones. Small pointed nose,
small mouth. Longish black-brown hair, which she sometimes knots up, to give herself more height.
Miriam.

On the day after she has her curious intimation of violence in
the dusky church, Miriam and the others go out to the ruins
at Monte Albán in a hired car, with a guide. Magnificently
preserved flattened stone pyramids, rising up from the broad
flat plain, at mystical intervals.

On their way home, driving along the Pan-American highway, approaching the city of Oaxaca, they see an ambulance

stopped just ahead of them, and a small cluster of people. Miriam begins to hold her breath.

"A woman and a baby, both killed," their guide mutters. He is sitting in front, next to the driver—but how did he know this, Miriam later wonders. He could see ahead? See the feet?

The car slows down, and Miriam, who is closest to the window on the left, looks out and sees: on the ground, a white cover of some sort pulled over two human shapes, one medium-sized, one tiny. Two thin brown ankles protruding from the larger shape. Dusty brown feet. Red streams coming from underneath the cover. Blood.

Sadness, misery on all the dark surrounding faces, the clustered onlookers. Their driver is very upset, although he goes on driving, slowly, as though in a mourning procession. To the guide, or perhaps to himself, he speaks in a low, continuous way, very softly, in Spanish.

Miriam also speaks to herself, but inwardly, with no sound. People are killed every day, in one way or another, somewhere, she tells herself; you must not sentimentalize these two, they are out of pain now. You did not know them.

Joan says, "That's absolutely horrible." Her mouth twists, and tightens.

And Eric, in a bitter voice: "They think God will get them across highways." He is looking anxiously at Miriam. To reassure him she smiles, and touches his hand.

Ten or fifteen minutes later, Joan speculates, "It could have been an older sister carrying a baby. There seem to be a lot of them—older kids helping. Family support systems."

Eric: "Sometimes it's hard to tell who's the mother, girls having babies at fifteen or sixteen." Eric is in favor of zero population growth, generally. Miriam would like to have one child. Early on in their marriage she was pregnant, accidentally, and she had a miscarriage: a lot of pain, blood. She still hopes for a child, eventually, but they no longer talk about it.

During the rest of that day Miriam, anyway, thinks often of the family of those killed people. She imagines a small funeral parlor, too many bright flowers. People sitting around, moaning, crying. She can see it all quite clearly.

Their ultimate destination is Ixtapa, for a rest, but they will get there by way of Puerto Escondido, a smaller, less well known resort. (It was Miriam who came up with the idea of Escondido: a young woman she knows in Seattle, a weaver with a stall in the Pike Place Market, has said it is beautiful, wonderful, undiscovered.) On maps it looked as though both those laps—Oaxaca to Escondido, Escondido to Ixtapa (skirting Acapulco)—were possible by car; their travel agent also believed that they could drive, although she cautioned them about bad roads. However, it turns out in Oaxaca that the only way to Escondido is by plane. A DC-3.

Miriam, of course, is the nervous flier of the group. It is explained to her that although the DC-3s are small and old, from the Second World War, they are (undoubtedly) kept in very good shape; after all they make the trip every day. Russell, who was a Navy pilot, cannot resist teasing; he says, "I can't imagine a trip on a DC-3 with no parachute. We always had parachutes."

Joan and Russell laugh, watching Miriam. She laughs, too, though unconvincingly.

However, as a farewell to their Oaxaca hotel, they have Margaritas in the bar, just before departure. Miriam has two, purposefully, and she loves that plane trip.

They fly very low over sharp green mountains that are

crisscrossed with tiny, narrow perilous roads, so low that each tree is visible, and occasionally there is a small village, a scattering of shacks. Tiny people are walking around—she can even see them as they look up at the plane.

"Oh, it's really beautiful!" says Miriam, several times; she is a little drunk.

"Miriam thinks that flying low is safer: it's closer to the ground," Eric explains to the others, who laugh. But that is just what Miriam does think, and she continues to believe it.

The view from their hotel room is exceptionally beautiful: a long broad white beach, deserted, beside the glittering, bright blue-green sea. Some strange greenish-gray vegetation and, at the far end of the beach, some white cliffs, or dunes—high, deeply ridged.

"Oh, how lovely," Miriam breathes; she is feeling the Margaritas, a little.

Behind her, Eric is saying, "This is the dirtiest room I've ever seen."

Miriam turns to see that he is right: an unmade bed, glasses with inches of dark liquid at their bottoms, floating cigarette stubs. A smeared mirror (lipstick? blood?), deep dust on the floor.

They both are right, about the view and the condition of the room.

It is quite a while before a maid comes in to clean it up, although Eric goes out to the desk to make a fuss.

For whatever reasons—fatigue, drinks, the flight—Miriam has a headache as she and Eric go to bed that night. But women cannot say that anymore, she knows, when they are not in the mood to make love. "I have a headache": a sitcom joke. And so she does not say it, and they do, happily—a happy surprise.

Downstairs in the hotel, and outside, some sort of fiesta seems to be going on. A rock band, as well as mariachis. Amplified.

All night.

The hotel is up on a high bluff above the sea—as they did not quite realize the day before, on their arrival. Its broad grassy grounds stretch to an edge, a dropping off. There is a round blue swimming pool and a thatch-roofed bar. A romantic situation for the central building, which is itself romantic, with its balconies and long arched windows, its heavy growth of bougainvillea—brilliant blossoms, delicate green vines.

However, the fiesta of the night before has left an incredible litter everywhere—piles of empty bottles: Scotch, French champagne, Mexican beer. Heaped-up ashtrays. Dirty plates.

Observing all this, around noon, Russell severely remarks, "Do you realize that no one has touched this since last night?"

And Joan: "Ugh. They're probably all home sleeping off hangovers. They just don't give a damn."

Perversely, Miriam finds something appealing, romantic even, in all that mess (although she does not say so, of course). So much champagne everywhere—what an incredible time they all must have had! It is how Gatsby's lawns must have looked after one of his parties, before the servants came.

But at that hotel, in Puerto Escondido (not West Egg), no one comes to clean up, not all day.

The ocean water—which holds, surrounds, embraces Miriam as she swims, and dives down to explore beneath its surface— is like no other water in her life; surely not the New England ponds of her childhood, or the harsh Atlantic waves that pound the Northeastern coast. This clear and lightly cool green water seems another element—enchanted water—and, swimming there, in the gentle waves, Miriam feels herself transformed, her body as quick and light as a minnow. As small and brown.

The others, Eric and Joan and Russell, are swimming there, too, but they are off somewhere else; Miriam hears them, distantly. She feels most splendidly, luxuriantly alone in the lovely water. And she is alone, except for a little Mexican boy, a child, who from time to time swims up to her; he smiles shyly, darkly, and as quickly disappears, another fish.

"Miriam, come on, we're getting out now," she hears someone call.

"I think I'll stay in for a while. I'll meet you up at the room."

"Well—"

She dives down as far as she can, in the watery green silence.

Late that afternoon, they learn that there are no rental cars available, and anyway it is not allowed to drive rented cars from Escondido to Ixtapa, or even to Acapulco.

Airplanes do not fly to Ixtapa, or to Acapulco. Only backward to Oaxaca.

There is only the second-class bus to Acapulco, and from there they may take a first-class bus to Ixtapa. One must travel from the second- to the first-class bus station, a matter of no distance. First class is called Estrella de Oro. A good sign.

"But, uh, couldn't we possibly just stay on here? It's really nice, don't you think? And second-class busses—" It is of course Miriam who has said all this.

She is answered by a chorus: "Oh Miriam, of course not, we have reservations, Ixtapa . . ."

Because they get there early, well before nine in the morning, they all have good seats on the bus, Miriam and Eric across the aisle from Joan and Russell, the two women at the windows.

They are the only North Americans on the bus.

The Mexicans who crowd into the other seats, and who, at the first and all subsequent stops, begin to fill the aisles, are not the poorest Mexicans—after all, they are travelling second class, not third—but they are considerably less rich than the four *norte-americanos*. Their clothes, the Mexicans', are bright and cheap and new, possibly bought for this trip, in some cases, whereas the North Americans wear old jeans and old cotton shirts; their leather bags are hidden in the luggage compartment, under the bus.

Miriam wishes that she were wearing something else. In these circumstances the jeans seem an affectation, besides being too hot. In a bright cotton dress, for instance (there are several in her suitcase, old summer favorites), she could look like any other passenger. She feels not liked by the Mexicans.

In addition to stops at all the small villages for new passengers, the bus is often forced to stop for sheep and cattle, or goats that appear in small herds or scattered at roadsides, evidently just emerged from the rich green tropical growth that lines the way. At moments, through the thick palm trunks, a portion of the sea is visible, sharp blue, as quickly gone; mostly the road wanders up small hills and down into dried-out creek beds. A burdened beast, the heavy, packed bus lumbers and creaks over potholes as large as moon craters.

At the village stops the windows are opened, things to eat and drink passed back and forth; shouts, laughter, money exchanged. To Miriam it all looks very good: the fruit, dark meats, strange pastries. But no one, not her husband or friends, would approve of such exotic fare; she knows this perfectly well.

Joan has brought some soda crackers in a package, from some restaurant; she passes them across to Miriam and Eric. Miriam is actually quite hungry, and the crackers help a little, although they are stale.

The bus is supposed to arrive at Acapulco at three, but it does not—not until four—and so the six-hour trip has taken seven.

"Seven hours on a second-class bus! No one will believe this story," Russell says, once they have got out and are standing there, stretching, breathing in the hot, murky city air. But he is laughing; Miriam can tell that it will be a good story for him, later on. They will all laugh about it on later trips together—probably.

They are standing in an incredible area of broken paving, refuse, dirt, over which hordes of shabby people are rushing with their battered luggage, packages.

Now they pick up their own suitcases (easy to recognize) from the pile outside their bus; they head for the street, where taxis can be seen cruising by. At some distance, in another direction, they can also see a large building, which is probably the station. And Miriam cannot resist saying, "We'd probably do just as well to get on another bus right here."

"Miriam, you've got to be kidding."

"Another second-class bus? Come *on*."

However, as soon as they have piled into a taxi and told the driver that they want the first-class station, Estrella de Oro, to Ixtapa, he tells them that they will have much trouble. Many crowds, he says gloomily; they may not get to Ixtapa.

They all look at each other. "But we have to get to Ixtapa," Eric mutters. "We have reservations for tonight."

Downstairs in the Estrella de Oro station a large crowd surrounds the ticket counter that is marked Zihuatanejo-Ixtapa —all kinds of people, mostly Mexican. It seems impossible that so many people would want to go in just that direction at that moment, but there they are.

"I suppose some people live and work there," Miriam suggests.

The waiting rooms and restaurant are on the second floor. "Why don't you girls go back upstairs? No point in all of us waiting in line," Eric says.

By now, it is six o'clock, and there is, in theory, a bus that leaves at seven-thirty. But will there be room on it for all these people, plus four North Americans? Quite possibly not.

The upstairs restaurant is closed, it seems, for repairs, and so Miriam and Joan simply wander about, in an idle though nervous way.

At one point they go out to the front entrance and stand there, observing the garish, tropical, and infinitely dirty scene, the broken-down cars and the beggars, dark withered women with sleeping children in their arms. "I think Acapulco is the bottom of the world." Miriam shudders as she says this, in the thick infested heat.

"Oh, I've seen worse," Joan says. She has recently been to India—a medical conference—which is presumably what she means.

Looking up at Joan, who is visibly tired, her light hair straggling down, her face dirt-streaked, lipstick gone, Miriam hopelessly thinks that Joan is still very beautiful, and then she wonders (not for the first time), But does Joan like me, really?

And then (a new thought), Oh, I just don't care!

After a while, they go back downstairs to see what has happened to Eric and Russell.

What has happened is that they have been given numbers and moved to another line.

"It's like a lottery?" asks Miriam.

Eric frowns. "Jesus, I hope not."

By about eight it is clear that they have missed the seven-thirty bus, but it is said that there is another at ten. Everything is shouted in Spanish, though, which they only partially understand, and they never actually see the busses as they come in or depart.

"Miriam was absolutely right," Eric concedes, in a rueful way. "We should have just gone into the second-class station and got on another bus."

Miriam does not quite remember having said that, but she supposes that she did.

Clear information comes through at ten-fifteen: they have indeed missed the ten-o'clock bus, but there is another at eleven. However, there are still many people who wait for the bus; that is evident.

"Eleven. Jesus, that gets us to Ixtapa about three, or *four*." Russell fumes.

"Terrific, that's what we really need right now. Five more hours on a bus. Even if it is first class." Eric is muttering, as though to himself.

In a low, very reasonable voice, Joan asks, "Do we have a choice, though? We'd never get into a hotel. Or could we?"

At which Miriam cries out, "Oh, no, God, not a hotel here
—it's so horrible! Why not just take a bus back to Escondido?"

She has spoken heedlessly, an outburst; still, she is unprepared for the silent, stony rage on those three so similar
faces, looking down at her from their impressive heights.
Joan's mouth is taut; Russell's eyes are wild, they glare as he
says, "That's crazy."

At which Eric turns from Miriam to Russell, as he says,
very quietly and furiously, "That's enough, now, Russ. Just
shut up, will you?"

As though they had always hated each other, the two men
glare at each other for a moment that lasts forever, in the
throbbing, crowded, filthy alien room, in Acapulco.

At eleven, having hardly spoken, any of them, for the past
forty-five minutes, in a blind exhausted way the four of them
pile into the bus that has mysteriously appeared, out of the
night. There are, strangely, just enough seats for everyone.

Miriam has stumbled into a window seat, on the left of the
bus, next to the ocean, as they wind northward, up the coast.
If anything were to be seen, through the heavy darkness—if
there were a view, hers would be the best, and she feels a
miserable guilt over even that nonexistent advantage. She
also (miserably) feels responsible for their quarrel. Eric and
Russell never fight.

The road seems very smooth, on this stretch of the coast. No
potholes, but there are curves, which the driver takes at top
speed, so that several passengers, Miriam among them, gasp
aloud. Miriam thinks it quite possible that he could be drunk.
Why not, at this dangerous, unreal hour? They will all be
killed, she thinks, and then, so total is her discomfort, so deep
her unhappiness, she further thinks that she does not care if

they are. But please don't let me be the sole survivor, she earnestly prays, to someone.

Most people have fallen instantly, noisily asleep, despite the danger. Beside Miriam, Eric sleeps lightly, restlessly.

The dawn is dirty, yellowish, menacing. In the coconut-palm plantations, just now barely, grayly visible, the heavy fronds are too still, and the ocean, glimpsed at intervals, is flat and black, dangerous-looking.

"Does it ever storm down here?" Russell has leaned across the aisle to ask this question of Eric, just awake.

Miriam watches Eric as he frowns and speaks impatiently. "I don't know. Probably."

If any of them spoke Spanish it would all have been different, Miriam thinks. They would have understood what was being said in the station about the busses, and even, maybe, have grasped a little more about the terrible accident on the road: how the guide knew so quickly what had happened, and what their driver was saying to himself—so sadly, so brokenly.

She will study Spanish, she then swiftly decides. There is a night course at the library branch at which she works; she will sign up as soon as they get home.

At about 5 a.m. they arrive at Ixtapa: a cluster of thick pale high buildings (an eruption of poisonous growths, Miriam thinks) in the sulfurous light. Across the way an endless golf course spreads, the smooth grass now all silverish gray.

They enter a building; there are red tiles, wooden arches hung with cut-tin ornaments.

From behind the desk a sleepy clerk hands out room keys.

In a heavily carpeted, perfectly silent elevator they all ascend.

Miriam and Eric's room has a gigantic bed, thickly quilted in red and orange. Two big chairs, and on the walls several huge garish paintings, of improbable bright flowers. A mammoth mirror, all shining.

Beyond exhaustion, they each in a perfunctory way wash up; they remove a few clothes and fall into bed.

Lying there, in the yellowish semi-dark, Miriam has a vivid sense of having arrived at last in hell. Beside her, Eric has gone instantly to sleep; his heavy breath rasps, regularly. She closes her eyes, but then uncontrollably re-sees, with perfect clarity, that tragic roadside scene—the covered bodies, blood, the protruding brown bare dusty feet.

Quickly opening her eyes, she feels that all her senses are conspiring to make sleep out of the question; she is so over-tired, so hungry, so afraid. She lies there for a while, eyes wide.

When she closes her eyes once more, however, Miriam has quite another vision: she sees herself on the second-class bus again, but she is headed back toward Escondido, and this time she's wearing a cotton dress, her bright blue, and she is alone. The bus rumbles along, much faster this trip, although from time to time it stops for passengers, and once more windows are opened, food passed through. And Miriam eats, everything she wants! Spicy aromatic meats and flaky pastries, pulpy fruits and tall sweet, colored fruity drinks. All exotic, delicious. And at Puerto Escondido the grounds have been all cleaned up; here and there are clumps of tropical vegetation, flowering bushes, small trees. And then the hotel itself, with its lovely bright covering bougainvillea.

Her room is clean and bright. She puts her bag down, undresses quickly, puts on her bathing suit and sandals. Grabs up a towel.

And she rushes, at last, down the winding rooted pathway, almost stumbling in her hurry—to the beach! She runs across the sand, to the gently lapping, warm clear water.

Half waking from what she recognizes as a dream (but how real it was, the water against her skin), Miriam tries, and fails, to read its meaning. Further awake, she realizes, too, that she is refreshed, as though she had indeed dipped into the ocean, or certainly had slept for more than the couple of hours which is actually the case.

Eric is still asleep. Carefully she slips out of bed and goes over to the window; she parts the heavy gold-threaded draperies and looks out. The menacing dawn has become an overcast, gray day, with strange dark clouds at the horizon. Closer in, on the beach, dozens of people are lying out on towels, body to body almost, all oiled as though there were sun—or as though they were dead.

Miriam unpacks some toilet things and goes into the bathroom, into further garish opulence: thick green towels, glistening green tile. And everything is scented, so sickly sweet that she hurries through washing.

Distantly, from the bedroom, she hears a knock at their door, in Russell's familiar rhythm—then Eric's sleepy voice, and Russell's. The closing door.

When she reënters the room Eric is sitting on the edge of the bed. He is still mostly unwashed, of course, his face blue-shadowed, blond stubble on his chin and his cheeks. But he looks cheerful, restored to himself. "A great place, huh?" he asks her. "Finally." And then he says, "Well, Joanie and Russ think a swim might be just the thing."

"Let them go swimming, then." Miriam has spoken with a calm, an assurance, that is absolute. "I think it looks dangerous." Let them drown, she does not say.

In her blue robe she goes over to stand beside him. She says, "I have to leave here." At that moment she is taller than he is.

He looks up at her, worriedly, uncomprehending. "You mean, just us?"

"I don't care. I have to leave."

Intelligent Eric has almost understood her, though. Reaching for the phone, he says, "I'll try for an afternoon plane," and he smiles, his old blond dazzling smile. "In the meantime, you don't want a swim?"

"No, I don't. But you go on, if you want to," and she smiles back.

Miriam. A small woman, who can suddenly, vividly see her husband Eric's body washed up on a beach, blond hair spread against cold sand, and long pale legs crookedly stretched down to the murky, turbulent sea.

Elizabeth

For every reason, including conventional wisdom's dictates that one should not go back to the scene of exceptional past happiness, I did not at all want to return to the Mexican beach at which I had not only been happy, my whole inner balance had seemed restored to me there, there at the extraordinarily lovely beach, with Elizabeth, my friend who now was dying and whom I could in no way restore, or save.

Since Elizabeth is—was about thirty years older than I am you say that her role in my life was maternal; my mother, a psychoanalyst, as my father is, does say just that; she is also aware of her own jealousy of Elizabeth—of course she is, both jealous and aware. To me that is not how it seemed at all; I did not see Elizabeth as "mother"; I simply liked her, and I admired her more than anyone I knew. For a long time I wondered whether my feelings for Judson, to whom I now am married, were colored by the fact that I first met him in her house. I have concluded that yes, they were, and are; after all, they loved each other too. Elizabeth and Judson.

In any case I did not at all want to go back to Mexico, to the beach and to Elizabeth's house, where now my friend lay miserably dying, of emphysema. And I knew at last that

I had to go, although of course Elizabeth did not say so—Elizabeth, the most elegantly tactful, most graceful of all people. I had been conscientiously writing her at least a couple of times a week, since she had allowed me to know of her illness, and for a while I managed to convince myself that that was better; many warm "interesting" letters might be less disturbing to her than an actual visit.

Then Judson, with whom I was not exactly in touch at that time—our connection was tentative, indefinite, perhaps anomalous—Judson telephoned me from Iowa, where he was living and teaching that year (Judson is a poet; I am a lawyer and I live—we live in Oakland, California). Judson said that I had better go down to see Elizabeth.

"It's simple, Minerva," he said. "If you don't you won't see her again."

Judson's poetry is minimalist, nor in personal conversation does he tend to waste words. I probably waste most things, certainly time and energy. Sometimes friendship, or love.

I asked him, "Will you go too?"

"If I can."

Judson and I had talked a lot, becoming friends, that first summer at San Angel, and once we had kissed. Not what anyone would term an affair, or even a "relationship"; still, the kiss took it a little out of the pure friendship class.

But I think I should begin with meeting Elizabeth, all those years back, the August when I was house-sitting for my parents in the hills of Berkeley. Being shrinks they both always took August off, and they usually rented a house in Wellfleet, Mass., where they got to see a lot of other shrinks. Then as now I was living in Oakland, and at that time I was going to law school, at U.C., in Berkeley. And so it made sense to stay in my parents' big house during August, to take care of their plants and the pool. They even offered to pay me, which I proudly refused.

At some point, along with various instructions, in an afterthought-sounding way my father said, "Oh. Your mother and I met an interesting woman at the Garsons'. An art historian. Originally Viennese, I think. She's renting the Jefferson cottage up the street and we told her to come use the pool if she ever felt like it." Piously he added, "Of course we told her to call you first."

"Dad. Really." My father knew perfectly well that I was having a relationship with a lawyer who was married but who spared me an occasional afternoon.

"Well, as you know it'll probably be cold all August anyway. How often we wonder whatever made us dream of putting in a pool. She might very well never call. Anyway you might like her."

If anyone else talked like that my father would call it "cross-signalling," which I believe is supposed to be "schizophrenogenic," but in himself he does not, of course. And in fact I am not especially schizy, more given to depression, unfortunately—although schizes probably don't much like their condition either.

"Her name is Elizabeth Loewenstein," my father added, and he repeated, "I really think you might like her. She has a very beautiful voice."

Only that last statement came as a surprise. Funnily enough, in view of his trade, my father is not at all a good listener, and so I was struck by the notion of a voice so beautiful that he would listen to it.

As things turned out, he was wrong only about the weather of that August, which was record-breakingly warm and clear, amazing and beautiful. From my parents' giant picture windows I watched the sun set over San Francisco and the bay, all implausibly gold and glistening.

Elizabeth Loewenstein, the possibly garrulous nuisance whom I had feared never phoned, and it is hard to recall on just what impulse I finally called her and asked her over for a swim. Partly it was because I was lonely—were I a believer, though, I would say that God had instructed me. As it is I see my call to her as a piece of sheer good luck, for me. In any case, I did call, and she said that yes, she would like to come over for a swim.

Elizabeth was small and dark, with short, graying curly hair and gray-green eyes. Lightly lined pale skin, a bony nose. Her manner was tentative, rather shy—and she had the most attractive voice that I had ever heard. (It was almost annoying, to have my father proved so accurate.) A low voice, slightly hoarse, and very slightly accented. A voice with great range: warm brightness, and a complicated depth of shadows. "Your voice has chiaroscuro," I once said to Elizabeth, and she laughed, of course, but she was pleased. She had a certain, highly characteristic way of saying "Ah!" like a tiny bark. That "Ah" was one of her responsive, listening sounds; she listened more actively than anyone, I thought—I think so still. She smoked a lot.

God knows what we talked about, that first afternoon. I only remember liking her very much and urging her to stay. She left after less than half an hour, and I told her please to come back whenever she could.

Nor do I remember much of the content of later conversations; it is rather the quality of being with Elizabeth that I remember. And her voice, and that tiny barked "Ah!" And her just-hoarse laugh.

Rather little of our talk was personal. Elizabeth almost never talked about herself, and so I was not encouraged to do so—which, that summer, was quite all right with me; I was tired of talking or even thinking about my troublesome, somewhat sordid love affair. Elizabeth often talked about places, her passion for Venice, and for the hill towns of Umbria and Tuscany. And she told me about the extravagant, wildly impractical (not even quite legal) gesture of buying a house in Mexico, near the beach.

Once I talked to a Berkeley woman who also admired and liked Elizabeth, and that woman said, "Oh, Elizabeth is so wonderful. You can do absolutely anything you want around her. Say anything."

Well, that was entirely to miss the point of Elizabeth, I thought. I would never knowingly have expressed a trivial or mean-spirited thought to Elizabeth; her own elegant, supremely intelligent demeanor forbade it. And actually one of the reasons that I so much liked Elizabeth was that she, as the phrase goes, "brought out my best." With her I was less trivial and mean, and much more intelligent, more finely observant than usual, and if not elegant at least restrained. Judson and I have talked about this, and he says that he felt the same. "Elevated," is a word he used. "Ennobled, even," Judson said.

This is the much abbreviated story of Elizabeth's life, as I pieced it together from stray remarks, tiny glimpses over our years of conversation, and all our letters.

She was born not in Vienna but in Paris, and later, before the Anschluss, she had studied in Vienna. Her parents were deported to camps in Germany, where they died (very little about this from Elizabeth). After the war she studied in Florence, in Bologna, and at Oxford. In addition to those places she had lived in Lisbon and in Cuernavaca, and in her Mexican beach town, San Angel. And in New York and

Boston. She had been married three times, twice divorced, once widowed—but of those relationships I know nothing. Once she spent some time at Lake Tahoe with a man who was trying to get a divorce in Reno but did not (out of character, this intimate glimpse arrived in a letter, like a present, when she knew that I was having some troubles of that nature). When I first knew her she was living in Boston, out in Berkeley on a studying visit. Later she moved down to New York. And later still, she moved to San Angel, to her small house in the manzanita thickets. For good.

That first summer in Berkeley Elizabeth and I saw each other mostly for late afternoon swims. We also went to the Berkeley and the Oakland art museums. Elizabeth looked as actively as she listened, as intently. I can see her: a small woman in something elegantly plain, gray linen, maybe brown, bending forward to see yet more clearly, her eyes narrowed in the effort, as she stands before a big canvas of some enormous, primitive animals, by Joan Brown.

Elizabeth was especially fond of that Oakland museum; to my great pleasure she preferred it to the San Francisco MOMA. "So much less pretentious," she remarked, quite accurately, I thought. "A more *real* museum, and architecturally it is marvellous, a beauty."

I have said that most of my talk with Elizabeth was impersonal; however, I do remember one conversation which became intimate, oddly enough having to do with our noses.

I had spent too many hours the week before just lying beside the pool, ostensibly studying for the bar, actually worrying about my life, as I enjoyed the sun. As a reward for that self-indulgence my nose first blistered, then peeled (I have inherited my mother's white Irish skin, my father's Polish-Jewish nose).

"I wish it would peel away," I said to Elizabeth, as though

joking. "Peel down to a tiny snub nose, like my mother's. Why did I just get her skin?"

Elizabeth laughed, accepting my joke, but she said, "You're too tall for a tiny snub nose, Minerva. Besides, yours is distinguished, like an Italian Renaissance lady." And then she sighed. "But I know about hating noses. For years I despaired of mine. And Minerva, I had more reason, you will admit. I am a very small woman with a very large nose."

"But yours is beautiful!"

"Ah! There, you see?"

We both laughed then, in the end-of-August almost cooling air, an hour or so before the sun would set.

In September Elizabeth went back to Boston. My parents came home, and I moved back into my own small Oakland apartment; I studied hard, I spent time with friends and with my lover, with whom I quarrelled a lot—on whom I made, according to him, impossible demands.

And I began what was to become a rich and wonderfully gratifying correspondence with Elizabeth. (I have it still, now boxed and tied up with heavy string. I always mean to take it out for rereading, but so far I have not.) It turned out that for us both letters were a form of conversation. I have sometimes even thought letters more satisfactory and God knows safer than most human contact, and it is possible that Elizabeth felt so too. In any case we wrote to each other quite often, and generally at some length. Only on trips Elizabeth might confine herself to postcards, with beautiful pictures: Venice, Spoleto, Siena.

And even cards from Elizabeth had the unique, quite unmistakable sound of her voice. I have sometimes had quite the opposite experience, very likely everyone has: the stiff, ungiving letters from friends who in person are both warm and amusing; dull letters from people one thought bright. Elizabeth's letters and her cards were exactly like herself, including her very slight, to-me-delightful mistakes in English.

Then, over the next months and the following years everything in my life went black, and wrong. I had passed the bar, and got a job with an okay firm in Oakland, specializing in labor law; but I felt that I was overworked, too many sudden trips to Chicago or Los Angeles, for depositions. Worse, I began to have serious doubts about the law itself, or rather about its current practice, its practitioners. My lover left for New Haven, with his wife. I got along with my parents even less well than usual, and I quarrelled in a serious way with a couple of longstanding friends. I was very tired. I imagined myself as a piece of old elastic, all gone gray, all the stretch and give worn out.

Well, a classic depression, but no one's depression seems "classic" to the person enduring it. And in my case, such overexposure to shrinks made it hard for me even to think, This is a depression, this too will pass. I did not even consider the possible aid of some therapy.

The very weather that year seemed inimical: a long fall and winter of cold rain, ferocious winds, followed by a spring of no respite but more cold and winds, a perpetual black-gray fog, looming up from the bay.

I had not written to Elizabeth that I was depressed, or whatever I was, but she may of course have sensed it. I did write about the frightful summer weather, the dark fog and cold, the perpetual wind.

Elizabeth wrote back that she would be in her house in Mexico for all of November, and that I must get some time off and come to visit her then. "I know how it is with long cold summers," she wrote. "You believe them to last forever, as sometimes they do. But maybe the idea of a warm white beach and many flowers will help a little to get you through the next few months." She further explained that she had already promised "such guest quarters as there are" to another friend—"a poet, Judson Venable, you might sometime have read him?" I had not.

But that is how I came to spend two weeks of that November in Mexico, my first trip to Elizabeth's house. Which in many ways changed my life.

As though to test my stamina, even September and October, which are often the nicest months in Northern California, that year were terrible; black heavy rains, and more rains, with dangerous flooding, mudslides near the coast. Dark, relentless winds. I packed for Mexico in a state of disbelief, jamming the light cottons recommended by Elizabeth into my seabag. And I boarded the plane that dark November morning still unconvinced that weather anywhere would be welcoming, and warm.

After seven hours that were alternately boring and turbulent (more tests!), including a frantic, high-stress changing of planes in Mexico City, in a smaller plane we flew toward a range of sharp green mountains, between perilously rocky peaks and over jungles, levelling at last toward a flat blue sea, and beaches. A white airstrip surrounded by green jungle growth.

Getting off that plane and walking down the ramp was like entering another atmosphere; I swam into warm, moist, delicately scented air, into an embrace of warmth and flowers. I began to smile, and for most of the time that I was there I felt that smile, which was interior as well—that November, and sometimes I did think how strange that it should be indeed November, the dark, funereal month of death and sorrow and ashes, especially in Mexico.

And—there was Elizabeth, small and lightly tanned, reaching up to kiss me on both cheeks, saying "Ah! Minerva, how good it is that you are here. But how thin, how pale! We must work to change you—"

I was embarrassingly close to tears, and only murmured that I was glad to see her too. I was grateful for the activity involved in stowing my bag into her improbably pink jeep. "I had not before driven a jeep, perhaps it is fortunate that it comes in so ridiculous a color," Elizabeth laughed, very happily.

We jolted over a deeply potholed road, through a shaded stretch of jungle, all wildly, diversely green, toward a small, shabby cluster of buildings, a town at which I barely looked, for there ahead of us was the sea: glinting, green and blue, white-waved, dancing out to a pale-blue sky. And everywhere flowers, bougainvillea, hibiscus, vines and bushes blooming in all possible shades, pinks and reds and purples, other blossoms of the smallest, most delicate yellow white. And butterflies, and birds.

"The place where you stay may not be entirely to your taste," Elizabeth was saying. "But you will be so little there. Mostly, it is very close to where I am."

She was right about my hotel, Del Sol: a cluster of bright new cottages around a pool and bar-restaurant—less than entirely to my taste. It was garish and sometimes noisy, populated as it was by young Texans and Germans. None of which mattered at all, as I was almost never there. That first day Elizabeth dropped me off with brief instructions. "You must take what time you need to collect yourself. Then walk out to the beach and turn left. Not too many yards to the end is a road leading up into the woods, and there you find my small house. It is brown, with a porch."

I collected myself for fifteen or twenty minutes, washing and changing to my lightest cotton dress, wrapping a bathing suit in a towel, and then I walked out to the beach and turned left. It is not too much to say that I already felt myself another person, in that air—Elizabeth's air.

Her house was not quite as easy to find as she had said. I hesitated in front of a couple of shacky cottages, and then I walked on up into some dark manzanita woods, the trees here and there overhung with heavy moss, thick vines. And there was Elizabeth's house—it had to be: a small square brown structure, over half its space a generous porch, the wall that faced the sea entirely of glass.

On the porch was a broad woven hammock on which someone obviously had slept ("Judson"?); there were rumpled pillows, a thrown-aside light blanket. Next to the hammock some big dark leather sling chairs.

And Elizabeth, coming out to greet me. "Ah, good Minerva to have brought your bathing suit. Always we have a little swim before our drinks and dinner."

Going inside, I saw that a large area between the house and the beach had been cleared, giving a branch-framed picture of the sea: sand, small birds, waves and distant headlands. The other walls were filled with pictures, narrow-framed line drawings, a few photographs. A wide low sofa, Elizabeth's bed (where sometimes she slept with Judson Venable?). Big bright wool pillows. A low tile table. Lamps.

I changed into my suit in the bathroom and we went down to the beach and swam, and I was entirely enchanted. Magic water, I thought, magically light and clear, of a perfect coolness.

I am aware, speaking of Elizabeth and of her surroundings, in San Angel, that I am presenting a possibly implausible perfection. As to Elizabeth herself, I can only say that for me she did seem that impossibility, a perfect person. To put it negatively, she was a person about whom I never felt even

slightly troubled, I was never bored with her—reactions that
I have experienced at one time or another with almost everyone else I have known very well (beginning, I guess, with
my parents). And as for San Angel itself, and the beach
there, it was at first perfect, perfectly quiet and beautiful.
Later it did change considerably, but that is the later part
of my story, of my return visit to Elizabeth, in her illness.

Back in the house, while I dressed Elizabeth began several
processes in the kitchen. "My good Aurelia comes later to
serve our dinner," she explained. "And Judson. He will very
soon be back, I think." She added, "I hope that you will like
him, as I do."

Actually I did not like Judson very much, at first. That
was in part because I assumed him to be Elizabeth's young
lover, and he seemed neither sufficiently young nor dashing
for that role. Also, he speaks very softly, and infrequently,
with an almost impenetrable Southern accent, which at the
time I took to be a bad sign, suggestive of bigotry, if not
downright stupidity.

Also, Judson is more than a little odd to look at. Tall, very
thin, with a big nose and big floppy-looking ears (curiously
we look somewhat alike, except for the ears; mine, like my
mother's, are quite small), as he shambled up to the porch
that first night I thought, Oh, surely not. I even thought,
Elizabeth, how could you?

I also distrusted Judson's protestations as to "their"
pleasure at my arrival. He said, "We've been most looking
forward to your visit," and the words sounded false and
stilted to me: the proverbial Southern good manners. I am
not notably trusting, in my reactions to people.

Aurelia, the Mexican helper ("maid" does not seem the
proper word, nor did Elizabeth ever refer to her as such)
Aurelia next arrived, and I did like her. She was tall and

iginal and splendid. We watched those displays each
we drank our salty-sweet Margaritas, served by Jud-
his particular Southern ceremoniousness, his semi-
he handed either of us our glass. Later, in the near-dark
we had our dinner. Later still, in the true dark, the
opical night, Judson would walk down to my cottage
. Sometimes we talked a little, more often not. He
ay good night, perhaps with a quick touch to my
my shoulder; I would go inside, get ready for bed,
for a little while. And Judson would hurry back to
h—or so I for the most part imagined.

y next-to-last night there, the end of my November
t my door Judson turned to me; he took my shoul-
his hands and then, quite simply, we kissed. Or, not
it was a complicated kiss, containing as it did so
spoken between us. In the next instant, that of our
n, I felt dizzied, almost unreal.

n touched my face. "You're lovely."

—" Meaning, as he knew, But what about you and
h?

nk you've got things a little wrong," was all he said.
im; talk about minimalism.

f the things I had wrong was the time of Judson's
, which took place quite early the next day; he was
the time I arrived for breakfast.

lly I was glad, happier to have a final day alone with
, and I did not want to face possible complications
lson. I wanted to thank Elizabeth, to say how happy
there had made me. And that is how it went; Eliza-
I talked and talked all day, she in her lovely, amaz-
. And she listened as I talked, with her wide, calm,
gray eyes.

he next day I went back to California.

· · ·

dark and beautiful, evidently deeply fond of Elizabeth; she
smiled a great deal and spoke almost not at all. (It turned
out later that it was through Aurelia that Elizabeth had
bought the house; it was actually in Aurelia's name, a legal
necessity, for beach-front property, but also generous on
Elizabeth's part. Aurelia's life was to be transformed.)

The sunset that was just then commencing over the far
eastern rim of the Pacific was the most splendid that I had
ever seen, the wildest range of color; gorgeous, brilliant rags
of color hung across the sky.

Judson made Margaritas which he served to us out on the
porch, as we watched the sunset remnants slowly fade—and
then Aurelia brought out our dinner, the first of many wonderfully garlicky fish.

But mainly, for me, there was Elizabeth's lovely voice to
listen to—although for the first time I began to wish she
would not smoke so much; I don't especially mind cigarette
smoke, not outside on a porch, but it obviously made her
cough a lot.

Elizabeth and I talked and talked, and talked and laughed,
and she smoked, and coughed. Judson said rather little, but I
had already begun to like him a little better. He had a good,
responsive smile, and his occasional laugh seemed warm.

After dinner Elizabeth looked tired, I thought; actually
I was too, and I got up to leave.

"Ah! Then Judson will walk with you," Elizabeth announced.

"Oh no, how silly, it's no distance—"

"Minerva, there could be banditos." Elizabeth laughed,
then a tiny cough. "But I expect you back here for breakfast, which we eat all through the morning."

And so Judson did walk back to Del Sol with me, along
the shadowy, gray-white sand, beside the black sea. In perfect silence. At my cottage door we stopped, and he touched

my shoulder very lightly. Not quite looking at me (a habit of his) he said, "I'm glad you came down." Adding, "She's really been looking forward to you." Long speeches, coming from Judson.

I was smiling as I went inside to bed.

Although I should admit to being quite as prurient as the next person, that November I did not subject the Elizabeth-Judson relationship to serious scrutiny, having to do with sex. I assumed some form of love to exist between them, and I did not concern myself with determining its exact nature. I saw that Elizabeth's bright gray eyes were often watching Judson thoughtfully, and that when he spoke she listened with her intensely attentive semi-smile. But then she watched me too, and listened when I spoke, with extreme attention.

My parents (the shrinks) would have said and probably did say that I had fallen into an ideal—or rather, an idealized situation: I was the loved child of loving parents, whose sexual lives I did not think about.

Another explanation for my relative lack of curiosity about them is that I was simply too happy there in Mexico, during that beautifully, caressingly warm November stay for serious thoughts about other people's lives. (An extreme of happiness can make you just as self-absorbed as misery can; witness people happily in love.) With Elizabeth and sometimes with Judson too I swam three or four times a day, in the marvellous, buoyant water; we walked, and walked and walked along the beach, in the direction of the tiny town, San Angel, or sometimes, more adventurously, we took the other direction: a walk that involved scrambling across small cliffs of sheer sharp rock, clutching in our passage at thin manzanita boughs, until we reached another beach, where we swam and sometimes picnicked.

An abundance of sheer phys
contributing to my new and
quite as significant was the ext
the white, white beach with its
jungle growth, interspersed v
foreground of a brighter, gree
And Elizabeth.

And Judson, whom I contin
began to think him good en
began to see the attractiveness
as he ambled along the sand,
the difficult stretch of rocks, c
to me, or to Elizabeth, who
times said (perhaps too often
up with young folks such as
out of breath; she required a
I put down simply to her age,
I thought Judson was very go
One of the pleasures of th
weeks in Mexico (as opposed
later)—a considerable joy for
shopping from the occasio
mostly, both men and wome
small children. They would h
us, trays of silver and jade;
our inability to make up our
Spanish, Elizabeth's considera
watched, and smiled, and see
Elizabeth bought a long da
rich and deep; I bought some
we both wore our new dresse

In those idle, happy ways o
ceeded each other, each brill

new, o
night a
son wit
bow as
shadow
heavy t
with m
would
arm, or
and rea
Elizabe
On
weeks,
ders in
simply;
much u
separati
Judso
"But-
Elizabet
"I th
So like
One
departu
gone by
Actu
Elizabet
with Ju
my time
beth an
ing voi
amused
And

Not quite predictably (I myself would not have predicted it) things went well with me, over the next months and then years that followed that November visit to Elizabeth. I was on an unusually even keel, for me. I had no major love affairs, nothing marvellous, but then no disasters either, just a couple of pleasant "relationships" with very nice men. I switched law firms, moving to a new one, still in Oakland, but a firm with a feminist-public good orientation.

Elizabeth and I wrote many letters to each other; I'm afraid mine were mostly about myself (Ah, the joys of a good correspondent as a captive audience!). Elizabeth wrote about everything except herself—or Judson, for that matter.

This went on until what must have been a couple of years later, when I got a letter from her that seemed more than a little alarming, though it was couched in Elizabeth's habitual gentle language. First, the good news that she had stopped smoking. And then this sentence: "Judson was here for a visit, and as I had not seen him for some time I fear he was alarmed by my not-so-good health."

Violently alarmed myself, I immediately telephoned Elizabeth; she was out at first, it was hours before I could reach her, and then, in character, she apologized for having upset me. "It is just this emphysema that I have," she said, but I could hear her labored breath. "Nature's punishment for heavy smokers." She tried to laugh, and gasped, and coughed.

After that I wrote to her much more often, and I tried to think of presents for her—not an easy task with elegant, apparently self-sufficient Elizabeth, but sometimes I succeeded, I think. I understood that she would write more briefly now, and less often, and that was true; she sent notes and postcards, thanking me for my letters, for whatever book or small Berkeley trophy I had sent (a paper cat, some Mexican-looking straw flowers). She said very little about how she was, but when I pressed her in a specific way ("Please tell me how you are") she admitted to not feeling very well. "I have so little strength, much discomfort. At times it seems cruel and unusual, at other times deserved." She would spend the winter in Mexico. "I hope there to breathe more easily."

This was the period I mentioned at the start, during which I believed, or perhaps succeeded in convincing myself that my frequent letters and small attentions were more beneficial than an actual visit from me would be.

And that was the theory broken by Judson's phone call, from Iowa, telling me that I should go to Mexico. "It's simple, Minerva. If you don't, you won't see her again."

"Will you go too?"

"If I can."

Those were the first sentences to pass between us since the night of that kiss, I later thought.

Of course I would go, and of course for every reason I did not want to. I made reservations, plane tickets and a cottage at Del Sol. Since Elizabeth had no phone down there I tried calling Del Sol myself, remembering that she received an occasional message through them. At last I reached a person who seemed to know that a Señora Loewenstein lived nearby, but I had no faith in the message, and I wrote to her too.

It was only as I boarded the plane, early one foggy, chilly morning at the San Francisco airport, that it occurred to me that this too was the month of November, that an almost exact four years had passed since my first visit.

However, disembarking at San Angel, the air was as moist, as caressing and fragrant as I remembered, and I began to think or hope that this trip might be all right.

I was surprised to find Aurelia in the terminal waiting room—tall, beautifully smiling Aurelia, who in answer to my quick question told me that Elizabeth was not well at all. "She lay down, she not get up," Aurelia said.

My first strong and confused reaction to this shocking news was anger: how could Elizabeth be so ill and not say so? Or, really, *how could Elizabeth be so ill?*

In Elizabeth's old pink jeep Aurelia drove me through the turbulent, violent green jungle, to the glittering sea, waves dancing in the bright mid-afternoon sunlight—to my cottage at Del Sol. I threw my bag onto the bed, threw water on my face and combed my hair, and ran back out to Aurelia, in the jeep.

How like Elizabeth (as Judson and I said later) to have arranged that my first sight of her should be reassuring. She lay on her hammock (Judson's hammock, as I thought of it), Elizabeth, in something pale blue, gauzy, very pretty. At my approach she half sat up, she reached out her hands to me. "Ah! Minerva. How good that you have come." And she smiled, and said all the rest with her eyes.

I bent or rather knelt to kiss her cheeks, thinking, How could I have blamed her for her illness? as I fought back tears. I asked, "You don't feel so well?"

"Not too." Another smile.

We had both begun to sound like Judson, I thought just then; our speech was as stripped down, as minimal as his was.

Elizabeth next asked, "Judson called you?"

"Uh, yes. He did."

She coughed. "He will come also?"

"He said if he could. He's really busy there, I think."

Her eyes blazed at me then, gray fire, for a full moment before she spoke, and when she did her damaged voice was wild. "He must come. You will call to him," she said.

I was too pummelled by violent emotion to understand, quite. I only said, "Of course. Tomorrow."

Elizabeth smiled, and she lay back and closed her eyes.
When she opened them again, after a short moment, it was
as though that passionate exchange had not taken place. She
said, "Ah, Minerva. Now you must tell me all about your
life."

Much later, Judson in his way explained, or nearly. "Yes, in
love. I think we were," he said. "But never lovers."

"But, why not?"

He smiled, not looking at me but at some private interior
vision, probably Elizabeth. "Too risky, for one thing. A good
friendship at stake."

By then of course Elizabeth had died, and Judson and I
in our own curious ways had "fallen in love" and married.
Which is what we both thought quite possibly she had
wanted us to do. In a sense I had been "offered up" to Judson,
that first November: Elizabeth's insistence that I visit her
just then, her always making Judson walk home with me.
Perhaps she thought that if he and I became lovers she would
love him less? I don't know, surely not, nor does Judson. It
is only clear that Elizabeth was an immeasurably subtle
woman, and a passionate one.

Now, more or less repeating things already said in letters, I
told Elizabeth that on the whole my life seemed very good.
I was happy in my new law firm, I was even getting along
better with my parents (possibly because they had separated
and were in that way getting along much better with each
other).

Elizabeth listened, and smiled, saying very little. Then
Aurelia reappeared, to arrange Elizabeth's pillows and to
say to me, "She very tired now, I think."

(Aurelia, soon to be the owner of that house; perhaps

something of that showed in her just perceptibly less shy bearing? Elizabeth must have liked to think of her there, of the difference in her life.)

I got up to go, but Elizabeth's thin hand detained me. "Dinner at eight," she said, with a smile and a small choked laugh.

It was still not late, not sunset time, and so instead of turning in at Del Sol I walked on down the beach, toward town. And I knew at once that this was a mistake: seemingly overnight (although actually there had been four years), big gaudy condominiums had sprung up, and a couple of huge hotels, towering and bright and hideous, where before there had been jungle green, and flowers, and space. Bodies crowded the beach; even had I wanted to walk much farther that would have been impossible. And vendors: I was almost instantly accosted by a swarm of them, sad-eyed little boys selling Chiclets, thin old men with bags of peanuts, women with the same butterfly-colored dresses as before, some trays of silver and jade, but I thought they all looked suddenly sad and thin, and too eager to sell, whereas before a certain diffidence had prevailed. The town's so-visible prosperity had not trickled down to these natives, I thought.

And so I turned back to Del Sol, and it was from my tiny sea-front cottage there that I watched the glorious sunset of that first night, and in fact of all the nights of my stay at San Angel—as from the bar loud hard rock music blared, hits from the States of ten or so years back. I could not decide whether the place had got much noisier in the years of my absence or if it was simply that I had spent so little time there, before.

At dinner Elizabeth looked rested, animated, though her color was so bad, yellowish, sallow. "I am glad you have

come!" she said to me several times—an unnecessary expense
of breath; I knew she was glad.

I went back to my cottage early, and read for a couple of
hours, despite the clamorous music—and I tried not to think
very deeply about Elizabeth.

The next morning was overcast, gray. I went in to the
office to put in the call to Judson, in Iowa, and I was told
that it would probably rain before noon. A surprise: I had
thought it never rained in San Angel.

A further surprise, and a better one, was that I got through
to Judson almost at once, with a perfect connection.

"I really think Elizabeth wants to see you," I told him. "I
think you should come down."

A small pause, during which I could hear him thinking,
almost. "Not right now," he said. "I can't. But tell her I'll be
there before Christmas."

"Good," I told him. "She'll feel better with something
definite." I added, "She's pretty bad."

"I know." Another pause, before he asked, "You're okay?"

"Oh, sure. But it's raining here."

He made an effort which I could feel to say, "Give my
love to Elizabeth."

"Oh, I will."

"Good-by, Minerva. I thank you."

"Good-by!"

In fact Elizabeth was to die before the end of November. She
had what I tried hard to think of as a merciful heart attack
a week after I had gone back to Oakland; Aurelia called to
tell me. As Judson and I said to each other, how perfectly in
character, how exquisitely polite of her to wait for death (for
which she must have longed, she was so miserably uncomfortable) until after I had come and gone, and to spare Judson even making the trip.

Her death, I suppose, is what began to bring me and Judson together, though actually a teaching stint at Stanford was what brought him to California, and to me. Here we began to talk less about Elizabeth, more of ourselves. Very cautiously we began to be in love.

But that morning in Mexico, when I went to see Elizabeth, walking across the damp gray sand in the gentle rain—when I gave her the message from Judson she smiled as though she had all the time in the world for future visits, for receiving and giving love.

"Ah! Good," she said. And, in almost Judson's words, "I thank you, Minerva. You are good to me, you and Judson."

Sintra

In Lisbon, Portugal, on a brilliant October Sunday morning, an American woman, a tourist, experiences a sudden rush of happiness, as clear and pure as the sunshine that warms the small flowers near her feet. She is standing in the garden of the Castelo de São Jorge, and the view before her includes a great spread of the city: the river and its estuary, the shining new bridge; she can see for miles!

Her name is Arden Kinnell, and she is a journalist, a political-literary critic, sometimes writing on films; she survives somewhat precariously, although recently she has begun to enjoy a small success. Tall and thin, Arden is a little awkward, shy, and her short blonde hair is flimsy, rather childlike. Her face is odd, but striking in its oddity: such wide-spaced, staring, yellow-green eyes, such a wide, clearly sensual mouth. And now she is smiling, out of sheer pleasure at this moment.

Arden and her lover-companion—Gregor, the slightly rumpled young man at her side—arrived the night before from Paris, and they slept long and well, after only a little too much wine at their hotel. Healthy Californians, they both liked the long, rather steep walk up those winding, cobbled streets, through the picturesquely crumbling, red tile–roofed old quarter, the Alfama, up to this castle, this view of everything. Arden is especially struck by the sight of the distant, lovely bridge, which she has read was dedicated to the revolution of April, 1974, the so-called Generals' Revolution that ended fascism in Portugal.

The air is so good, so fresh and clear! Breathing in, Arden thinks, Ah, Lisbon, how beautiful it is. She thinks, I must tell Luiz how much I like his city.

Madness: in that demented instant she has forgotten that at a recent party in San Francisco a woman told her that Luiz was dying (was "terminal," as she put it). Here in Lisbon. Now.

And even stranger than that friendly thought of Luiz, whom she once loved wildly, desperately, entirely—dear God, friends is the last thing they were; theirs was an adversary passion, almost fatal—stranger than the friendly impulse is the fact that it persists, in Arden, generally a most disciplined woman; her mind is—usually—strong and clear, her habits of work exemplary. However, *insanely*, there in Lisbon, that morning, as she continues to admire and to enjoy the marvellous sweep of city roofs, the graceful bridge above the shining water, she even feels the presence of Luiz, and happily; that is the incredible part. Luiz, with whom she experienced the wildest reaches of joy, but never the daily, sunny warmth of happiness.

Can Luiz possibly just that day have died? Can this lively blue Portuguese air be giving her that message, and thus causing her to rejoice? Quickly she decides against this: Luiz is not dead, he cannot be—although a long time ago she surely wished him dead, believing as she then did that only his death could release her from the brutal pain of his absence in her life.

Or, could the woman at the San Francisco party (a woman

whom she did not like at all, Arden now remembers—so small and tautly chic), could that woman have been mistaken? Some other Luiz V. was dying in Lisbon? But that was unlikely; the woman clearly meant the person that Arden knew, or had known—the rich and well-connected, good, but not very famous painter. The portraitist.

Then, possibly Luiz was ill but has recovered? A remission, or possibly a misdiagnosis in the first place? Everyone knows that doctors make such mistakes; they are often wrong.

Arden decides that Luiz indeed is well; he is well and somewhere relatively nearby, in some house or apartment that she can at least distantly see from where she is standing, near the crenellated battlements of the castle, on the sun-warmed yellow gravel. She looks back down into the Alfama, where Luiz might be.

Gregor, the young lover—only five years younger than Arden, actually—Gregor, a photographer, "knows" about Luiz. Friends before they became lovers (a change in status that more than once has struck Arden as an error), in those days Arden and Gregor exchanged life stories, finding that they shared a propensity for romantic disaster—along with their similarly precarious freelance professions (and surely there is some connection? both she and Gregor take romantic as well as economic risks?).

"Can you imagine a woman dumb enough to believe that a Portuguese Catholic would leave his wife and children just for her?" Arden asked, in the wry mode that had become a useful second nature to her. "Oh, how stupid I was!" she lamentingly laughed. And Gregor countered with his own sad love adventure; she was a model, Lisa. "Well, can you imagine a photographer who wouldn't know not to take up with a model?" This was when Gregor, just out of art school, was trying to get a start in New York; Lisa, though younger than he, was already doing quite well. But Lisa's enchanting liveliness, and her wit, as well as her lovely thin body, turned out to be coke-maintained. "No one then was doing anything but plain old dope and a little acid," was Gregor's comment. "I have to hand it to her, she was really ahead of her time. But *crazy*."

Gregor too can be wry, or does he imitate Arden? She sometimes has an alarmed sense that he sounds like her, or tries to. But he is fun to talk to, still, and often funny. And he is smart, and sexy. Tall and light-haired, he is not handsome but very attractive, with his huge pale Russian eyes, his big confident body. A good photographer, in fact he is excellent.

At moments, though, Arden feels a cold enmity from Gregor, which is when she wishes that they were still "just friends." And is he an alcoholic, really? He drinks too much, too often. And does he love her?

Oh, *love*, Arden thinks. How can I even use that word.

Gregor and Arden do not in fact live together, and although she sometimes tells friends that she considers this an ideal arrangement, often she actually does not. Her own house in Larkspur is small, but hardly too small for two, and it is pleasantly situated on a wooded knoll, no other houses in sight. There is a pool, and what Arden considers her recreational garden, an eccentric plot all crowded with squash and nasturtiums and various lettuces. Gregor spends much of his time there with her; he likes to swim, although gardening does not interest him—but he also keeps a small place of his own on a rather bleak street near Twin Peaks, in San Francisco, high up in the fog and winds. And his apartment itself is bleak: three small rooms, monastically clean and plain and white. There is also a darkroom, of course, where he often works late at night. No personal traces anywhere, no comfortable mess. Forbidding. Arden has only been there twice. Even when they are in the city it always seems better to drive on back to Larkspur, after the movie or concert, whatever. But Arden thinks of him there, in those rooms, on the nights that he stays in town, and her thoughts are uneasy. Not only the existence of that apartment, an alternative to her house, as well as to herself, but its character is threatening to Arden, reminding her of aspects of Gregor himself: a sensed interior coldness, an implacable emptiness. When she thinks of Gregor's house she could be imagining an enemy.

She has never seen any food around, for instance: does he only drink there, alone, in his white, white rooms? She does not imagine that he sees other women, but certainly he could. He could go out to bars, bring women home. This though seems less likely, and therefore possibly less threatening than just drinking alone, so grimly.

At the end of Arden's love affair with Luiz there were hints in local gossip columns that he had a "somewhat less than professional relationship" with a few of the subjects of his portraits, and the pain of this information (explaining so much! so plausible!) was a further unbearable thrust to Arden.

In any case, since Gregor knows about Luiz, including the fact of Lisbon, home of Luiz (but not the possible mortal illness; Arden has not been able or perhaps not seen fit to mention this), does Gregor think it strange that so far in Lisbon Arden has not mentioned Luiz, whom she used sometimes to talk about? Here she has not once said his name, in any context. She herself does not quite know why she has not.

Still, just now she is happy, looking down to small balconies of flowers, of vines that climb up on intricate iron grillwork. She wonders: possibly, is that where Luiz lives, that especially handsome, long-windowed apartment? with the dark-gray drapery?

Arden is happy and well and suddenly very hungry. She says to Gregor, "Isn't that a restaurant over there? Shouldn't we try it? It looks nice, and I can't bear to leave this view."

"Well, sure." Gregor's look in Arden's direction is slightly puzzled—as well it might be, Arden thinks. She too is puzzled, very. She loves Lisbon, though, and her blood races dizzily.

They go into the restaurant; they are quickly seated at a white-clothed table, with the glorious Lisbon view.

"Had you ever, uh, heard about this place before?" asks Gregor, once their wine has come. This is his closest—if oblique—reference to Luiz, who surely might have mentioned to Arden a favorite restaurant, with its marvellous view. But as though realizing what he has done Gregor then covers up. "Or did you read about it somewhere? a restaurant guide?"

"No, actually not. It just looked good. The doors—" The front door is of heavy glass, crossed with pitted, old-looking iron bars. "An interesting use of glass, don't you think?"

"Yes," says Gregor.

Their eyes regard each other suspiciously.

Remembering Luiz, Arden sees flat smooth black hair, that shines, in bedside lamplight. She watches him as he dresses, while she lies there spent and languid; she watches everything shining, his hair and his bright black eyes, their dark glitter. He comes over to kiss her good-by, for that day, and then he cannot, does not leave.

"This is an illness, this endless craving that I have for you. A mania—" Luiz more than once remarked, with an accuracy that Arden could not then admit to herself. She did not feel ill, only that all her nerves had been touched, involved.

Luiz is (or was) an excellent portraitist. His paintings were both elegant and penetrating, often less than flattering; on the other hand, on occasion, very flattering indeed. He was at his best with women (well, of course he was, Arden has thought). Once she went to an exhibit of his paintings at a Sutter Street gallery—though not, naturally, to the opening, a social event much reported in the papers.

In fact they first met at a gallery opening. From across the room Luiz found Arden (that is how he put it, "I *found* you there"), coming over to talk to her intently for a while (about what? later she could never remember). He called the next day; he called and called, he would not be put off.

This was in the early sixties. Arden, then much involved in the peace movement, saw his assault on her life as an incursion, an invasion. He attacked with superior weapons, and with the violence of his passion for her. And he won. "I think that you have fallen in love with my love for you," he once (again accurately) remarked.

Out of her depth, and dismayed by everything about Luiz —the wife and family at home in Portugal, a fascist country —Arden found some small comfort in the fact that all his favorite writers seemed to be of the Left: Silone, Camus— and that his favorite movie director was Pasolini.

She pointed this out, rather shyly—the shyness of an essentially defeated person.

"My darling, I have a horror of the Right, of *fascismo*."

(But in much the same tone he also said, "I have a horror of *fat*," as he stroked her thin thigh, then cupped the sharp crest with his wise and skillful hand.)

You could simply look at his eyes, or his mouth, Arden thinks now, and know that Luiz was remarkable.

She remembers his walk. The marvellous confidence in that stride. During all the weeks of suffering so acutely from his absence in her life (classically, Luiz did not get the promised divorce, nor did he defect from the fascist government he railed against; he went back to Lisbon, to his wife, to that regime)—during all that time of suffering, it was the thought of his walk that caused Arden the most piercing pain: that singular, energetic motion of his body; its course through the world, without her.

After lunch, much more slowly than earlier they had climbed the streets, Arden and Gregor start down. The day is still glorious; at one point they stop at a small terrace where there are rounded cypresses, very small, and a lovely wall of soft blue tiles, in an intricate, fanciful design—and a large and most beautiful view of sky and majestic, glossy white clouds, above the shimmering water of the sea. From this distance the commemorative suspension bridge is a graceful sculpture; catching the sunlight, it shines.

Arden is experiencing some exceptional, acute alertness; as though layers of skin had peeled away, all her senses are opened wide. She sees, in a way that she never has before. She feels all the gorgeous day, the air, and the city spread below her.

She hardly thinks of Gregor, at her side, and this is something of a relief; too often he is a worrying preoccupation for her.

Their plan for the afternoon has been to go back to their hotel, where they have left a rental car, and to drive north to Cascais, Estoril, and Sintra. And that is what they now proceed to do, not bothering to go into the hotel, but just taking their car, a small white Ford Escort, and heading north.

As they reach the outskirts of the city, a strange area of new condominiums, old shacks, and some lovely, untouched woods—just then, more quickly than seemed possible, the billowing clouds turn black, a strong wind comes up, and in another minute a violent rainstorm has begun, rains lashing at the windshield, water sweeping across the highway.

Arden and Gregor exchange excited grins: an adventure. She thinks, Oh, good, we are getting along, after all.

"Maybe we should just go to Sintra, though," he says, a little later. "Not too much point in looking at beach resorts?"

Yielding to wisdom, Arden still feels a certain regret. *Cascais.* She can hear Luiz saying the word, and "Estoril," with the sibilant Portuguese *s*'s. But she can also hear him saying *Sintra*, and she says it over to herself, in his voice.

A little later, looking over at her, Gregor asks, "Are you okay? You look sort of funny."

"How, funny?"

"*Odd.* You look odd. And your nose. It's so, uh, pink."

Surprising them both, and especially herself, Arden laughs. "Noses are supposed to be pink," she tells him.

Normally, what Arden thinks of as Gregor's lens-like observations make her nervous; they make her feel unattractive, and unloved. But today—here in Portugal!—her strange happiness separates her like a wall, or a moat from possible slights, and she thinks, How queer that Gregor should even notice the color of my nose, in a driving rainstorm—here, north of Lisbon, near Sintra. As, in her mind, she hears the deep, familiar, never-forgotten voice of Luiz saying, "I adore your face! Do you *know* how I adore it? How lovely you are?" She hears Luiz, she sees him.

. . .

Then quite suddenly, as suddenly as it began, the storm is over. The sky is brilliantly blue again, and the clouds are white, as Arden thinks, No wonder Luiz is more than a little erratic—it's the weather. And she smiles to herself.

Suppose she sent him a postcard from Lisbon? *Ego absolvo te.* Love, Arden. Would he laugh and think fondly of her, for a moment? *Is* he dying?

In Sintra they drive past a small town square, with a huge, rather forbidding municipal building, some small stores. The wet stone pavement is strewn with fallen wet yellow leaves. They start up a narrow road, past gates and driveways that lead to just-not visible mansions, small towered castles. (The sort of places that Luiz might visit, or own, for weekends, elegant parties.) As they climb up and up in the small white car, on either side of the road the woods become thicker, wilder, more densely and violently green—everything green, every shape and shade of green, all rain-wet, all urgently growing. And giant rocks, great dead trees lying beside them. Ferns, enormously sprouting. Arden is holding her breath, forgetting to breathe. It is crazy with green, she thinks, crazy growth, so old and strong, ancient, endless and wild, ferocious. Like Luiz. Like Portugal, dying.

Gregor is making some odd maneuver with the car; is he turning around, mid-road? Trying to park, among so many giant rocks, heavy trees, and brilliant, dripping leaves?

In any case he has stopped the car. On a near hill Arden can see the broken ruins of a castle, jagged black fragments of stone, and in the sky big clouds are blackening again.

Willing calm (though still having trouble with her breath), Arden says, "I think it's going to rain again."

Huge-eyed, pale, Gregor is staring across at her. He says,

"You cut me out—all the way! You might as well be here alone!"

He is right, of course; she is doing just that, pretending he is not there. So unfair—but his staring eyes are so light, so *blue*. Arden says, "I'm sorry, really—" but she can feel her voice getting away from her, can feel tears.

Gregor shouts, "I don't know why we came here! Why Portugal? What did you expect? You could have just come by yourself!"

But Arden can hardly hear him. The rain has indeed begun again; it is pelting like bullets against the glass, and wind is bending down all the trees, flattening leaves.

And suddenly in those moments Arden has understood that Luiz is dead—and that she will never again feel for anyone what she felt for him. Which, even though she does not want to—she would never choose to feel so much again—still, it seems a considerable loss.

In fact, though, at that particular time, the hour of that passionate October storm (while Arden quarrelled with Gregor), Luiz is still alive, although probably "terminal." And she only learns of his death the following spring, and then more or less by accident: she is in Washington, D.C., for some meetings having to do with grants for small magazines and presses, and in a hasty scanning of the *Post* she happens to glance at a column headed "Deaths Elsewhere."

Luiz —— —— V. (There were two intervening names that Arden has not known about.) Luiz V. had died a few days earlier in Lisbon, the cause of death not reported. Famous portraitist, known for satire, and also (this is quite as surprising to Arden as the unfamiliar names)—"one of the leading intellectuals in Lisbon to voice strong public support for the armed forces coup in April 1974 that ended half a century of right-wing dictatorship."

Curiously—years back she would not have believed this possible, ever—that day Arden is too busy with her meetings to think about this fact: Luiz dead. No longer someone whom she might possibly see again, by accident in an airport, or somewhere. No longer someone possibly to send a post-card to.

That day she is simply too busy, too harried, really, with so many people to see, and with getting back and forth from her hotel to her meetings, through the strange, unseasonable snow that has just begun, relentlessly, to fall. She thinks of the death of Luiz, but she does not absorb it.

That quarrel with Gregor in Sintra, which prolonged itself over the stormy drive back to Lisbon, and arose, refuelled, over dinner and too much wine—that quarrel was not final between them, although Arden has sometimes thought that it should have been. They continue to see each other, Arden and Gregor, in California, but considerably less often than they used to. They do not quarrel; it is as though they were no longer sufficiently intimate to fight, as though they both knew that any altercation would indeed be final.

Arden rather thinks, or suspects, that Gregor sees other women, during some of their increasing times apart. She imagines that he is more or less actively looking for her re-placement. Which, curiously, she is content to let him do.

She herself has not been looking. In fact lately Arden has been uncharacteristically wary in her dealings with men. In her work she is closely allied with a lot of men, who often become good friends, her colleagues and companions. How-ever, recently she has rather forcibly discouraged any shifts in these connections; she has chosen to ignore or to put down any possible romantic overtones. She spends time with women friends, goes out to dinner with women, takes small trips. She is quite good at friendship, has been Arden's conclusion, or one of them. Her judgment as to lovers seems rather poor. And come to think of it her own behavior in that area is not always very good. Certainly her strangeness, her removal in Lisbon, in Sintra, was quite enough to provoke a sensitive man, which Gregor undoubtedly is.

On that night, the night of reading the news item (Deaths Elsewhere) containing the death of Luiz—that night Arden is supposed to meet a group of friends in a Georgetown restaurant. At eight. In character, she gets there a little early, and is told that she will be seated as soon as her friends arrive; would she like to wait in the bar?

She would not, especially, but she does so anyway, going into a dark, panelled room, of surpassing anonymity, and seating herself in a shadowed corner from which new arrivals in the restaurant are visible. She orders a Scotch, and then wonders why; it is not her usual drink, she has not drunk Scotch for years.

By eight-ten she has begun to wonder if perhaps she confused the name of the restaurant. It was she who made the reservation, and her friends could have gone to some other place, with a similar French name. These friends like herself are always reliably on time, even in snow, strange weather.

The problem of what to do next seems almost intolerable, suddenly—and ridiculously: Arden has surely coped with more serious emergencies. But: should she try to get a cab, which at this crowded dinner hour, in the snow, would be difficult? And if she did where would she go?

In the meantime, at eight-twenty, she orders another drink, and she begins to think about the item in the paper. About Luiz.

Odd, she casually thinks, at first, that she should have "adored" a man—have planned to marry a man whose full name she did not know. And much more odd, she thinks, that he should have publicly favored the '74 revolution, the end of dictatorship. Opportunism, possibly, Arden first thinks. On the other hand, is she being unfair, unnecessarily harsh? He did always describe himself as anti-fascist. And perhaps that was true?

Perhaps everything he said to her was true?

Arden has finished her second drink. It is clear that her friends will not come; they have gone somewhere else by mistake, and she must decide what to do. But still she sits there, as though transfixed, and she is transfixed, by a sudden nameless pain. Nameless, but linked to loss: loss of Luiz, even, imminently, of Gregor. Perhaps of love itself.

Understanding some of this, in a hurried, determined way Arden gets to her feet and summons the bill from her waiter. She has decided that she will go back to her hotel and order a sandwich in her room. Strange that she didn't think of that before. Of course she will eventually get a cab, even in the steadily falling, unpredicted snow.

My First
and Only House

Because of my dreams, I have begun to think that in some permanent way I have been imprinted, as it were, by the house in which I spent my first sixteen years. I have never owned another house (one could also say that I did not own that house either), and since this is true of almost none of my contemporaries and close friends in real-estate-crazed California, it would seem to deserve some explanation. Circumstances aside, is it possible that I have never bought or seriously thought of buying another house because of the strength of that imprinting, and if so, just why has it been so dominant, so powerful, in my life?

In more than half of my dreams I live there still, in that house just south of Chapel Hill. I am visited there in dreams by the present-day population of my life, people who in fact have never been to that hilltop where the house was—where it *is;* I saw it there last summer.

I also, though very rarely, dream of my former—my first and only—husband. But since this occurs only when I am angry with the man with whom I now live, the reasons for those dreams seem fairly clear. However, as with not buying another house, it also seems possible that I have not remarried because of that early impression of marriage. Californians, or some of them, might say that I avoid commitment, but that is not true. I do not. In fact, I seem to seek it out. I simply feel that first marriages, like the first houses in which we live, are crucially important, that in one way or another we are forever marked by them.

The Chapel Hill house, as my parents first found and bought it in the early twenties, a few years before I was born, was a small, possibly run-down and isolated farmhouse on a lovely broad hilltop. Very likely it was a good buy, cheap even for those pre-boom days; my father, as a just-hired professor at the university, would certainly not have had much money. In any case, my mother and father must have been drawn to all that space, a couple of acres; they may have already been planning the gardens, the tennis court and the grape arbors they were to put in later. And they must have fallen in love with the most beautiful view of farther gentle hills and fields, and a border of creek. They would have placed those aesthetic advantages above the convenience of a smaller lot, a tidier house in town. And along with the space and the view, they chose an unfashionable direction (which would have been characteristic; my parents—especially my mother, a snobbish Virginian—were always above such considerations).

Although in those days Chapel Hill was an extremely small town, there was already a row of fairly grand houses on Franklin Street, which continued on to become the Durham Road; whereas the highway running down past our house went on to Pittsboro, which was then a very déclassé town. And although our house became rather grand too in its way, there was always the Pittsboro connotation. "Oh, you live almost to Pittsboro," early non-driving beaux used to say to me by way of complaint about the distance they had to walk to get to my house, then back into town for a movie or whatever, back home with me, then back to wherever they lived, maybe Franklin Street.

By the time I was born, a small wing had been added to the old farmhouse, with a large upstairs bedroom for my parents and a small living room below. And that is what I first remember, that slightly lopsided house with the narrow front porch, a new wing on one side and on the other the tiny separate building that housed my father's study. In early snapshots the house looks bare, rather naked on its hilltop, with new, spindling trees out in front.

But what I most remember is flowers—everywhere. Roses, pink and white ones, climbed up a trellis and over the roof of the porch, entangled there with thick wisteria vines; rose petals and heavy lavender blossoms brushed the roof's green shingles and the ground. Over an arbor, next to the red-clay tennis court, more wisteria mingled with the gray-green grapevines—and then there was the garden itself: terraced beds of more rosebushes, crape myrtle and Japanese quinces, tall hollyhocks, sunflowers, cowslips, sweet william and lilies of the valley. Below the garden proper, beyond a green wooden fence, was a small apple orchard. Our family laundry was hung out there, billowing white sheets among the whiter apple blossoms.

In the side yard grew rows of irises and a bed of jonquils, a flowering plum tree, more quinces. That yard sloped down to a small, much steeper area of pinewoods above the swimming pool that my father put in during the early thirties with his World War I bonus. In those woods bloomed white dogwood and wildflowers—tiny, amazing wild irises and yellow dogtooth violets—nestled down among the dead pine needles and rotting leaves that covered the earth.

Of course it is highly unlikely—impossible, even—that all those flowers and shrubs and trees came to blossom at anywhere near the same time or even within a single season.

But that is what I remember: the flowers all in bloom and as taken for granted (by me) as the grass, as the sweeping view of hills and fields, of everything green—a view that no longer exists from that house.

I am writing, then, at least in part, about the vagaries of memory and about the house that in dreams I permanently inhabit—or, it might be more accurate to say, the house that inhabits me.

Indoors, even before the final ungainly additions to the house, some strangeness prevailed, some awkwardness as to proportion and transition from one room to another. Upstairs, there was even a dead-end hall and several completely nonfunctional closets. The final, large addition to the house was built where my father's study had been. This new wing included a big living room and a big new study for my father, a prominent feature of which was a locked liquor closet (Verlie, who worked for us, was thought to drink). Upstairs was a double bedroom for my parents, a guest room and a sleeping porch. In actual fact, my mother slept in the guest room and my father out on the sleeping porch, an arrangement that seemed perfectly normal to me at the time.

Other people, though, did remark on the size of that house for just three people. "Don't you all get lost in all these rooms?" was the standard question. I did not exactly see us as lost, but I do remember a not-quite-conscious feeling that my parents were too far away from where I slept; that they were also far from each other did not strike me as strange until sometime later.

Below us, in a small house down the hill (even closer to tacky Pittsboro), lived a family of six: two parents, four small children. Very likely they were truly needy people. I somehow learned, or heard, that they all slept together in one bed. And I felt the most passionate envy of that condition, that bodily family warmth. As I imagined it, they would all lie cuddled like puppies, with the mother and father on the outside edges, protectively.

For reasons I can no longer remember, I was moved about among those oddly shaped bedrooms in the old part of the house. I slept alone, of course, and was generally frightened at night—until I learned to read. Then, as now, books served to keep the terrifying world at bay for a while.

Downstairs was generally more cheerful than up; the house was splendid for parties, for bringing people home to. Everyone admired its impressive size and the splendid view. And we three difficult, isolated people got along much better when there were others around. Even Verlie, she who supposedly drank (my own view is that my father simply thought she might if tempted; it is what he thought Negro servants did), liked cooking for parties more than for just us three. So my parents entertained a lot, and later I was encouraged to also. "We love to have your friends here," I was always told.

Downstairs was better, but outside was better yet. Once we had the pool, that was where most of the parties were. People were always invited to "come by for a dip," drinks were brought down, and then the guests were probably encouraged to stay on for supper. At one end of the pool, a privet hedge shielded us from the road, and it flowered, intensely sweet.

Still, it is strange to me that I am so fixed, so literally rooted in a house of which my memories are not of a very positive nature on the whole, and standard psychological explanations of fixation by trauma seem both simplistic and uninteresting. Last summer, as I have said, I went to see the house, "my house," which I had not seen for twenty-five years, not since my father died and my stepmother, who had inherited it outright, put it up for sale (a serious trauma, that: it was made clear that indeed I had never owned the house, nor had my mother, who might as well have been a guest). And what is curious is that I cannot now, six months later, recall just how it looked. It had been repainted a new color. But was it gray? Pale yellow? I have no idea. (I recently saw my former husband in a local bank, and for one fleeting instant I did not know who he was, but I know very clearly how he looked thirty years ago.) Across the road from the house, though, I am sure that there was a total obstruction to the view. Huge trees, I think.

But that freshly painted, viewless house is non-existent in my mind; it is not where I live. I live in a huge, mad house with the loveliest view. With everything in bloom.

A NOTE ON THE TYPE

The text of this book was set on the Linotype in Garamond
No. 3, a modern rendering of the type first cut by Claude
Garamond (1510–1561). Garamond was a pupil of
Geoffroy Tory and is believed to have based his letters on
the Venetian models, although he introduced a number of
important differences. It is to him that we owe the letter
known as "old style." He gave to his letters a certain elegance
and feeling of movement that won for their creator an
immediate reputation and the patronage of Francis I of
France.

Composed by Maryland Linotype Composition Company,
Baltimore, Maryland

Printed and bound by Fairfield Graphics,
Fairfield, Pennsylvania

Designed by Cecily Dunham